Strong hands jerked her back to safety and against a rock-hard chest as the car flew by and into the intersection, narrowly avoiding a collision with two other cars before speeding away.

Trey's powerful arms wrapped around her and held her steady in the protective gap between two parked cars. Her body trembled as adrenaline poured through her, igniting her nerve endings.

"Are you okay?" Trey whispered against her ear. His warm, fresh breath spilled against the side of her face, and his reassuring squeeze calmed her.

"I'm okay." She turned in his embrace to meet his concerned gaze and cupped his cheek. *"Gracias."*

"Idiot kids racing," he said and shook his head.

Only, Roni was certain it hadn't been an idiot kid. "It was intentional, Trey."

LOST IN LITTLE HAVANA

New York Times Bestselling Author
CARIDAD PIÑEIRO

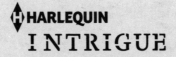

HARLEQUIN
INTRIGUE

Thank you to my lovely daughter, Samantha, for being my best
friend and such an inspiration. I am so proud of all that you've
accomplished with your writing and can't wait to see
what you do next.

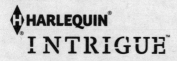

Recycling programs
for this product may
not exist in your area.

ISBN-13: 978-1-335-58231-7

Lost in Little Havana

Copyright © 2022 by Caridad Piñeiro Scordato

For questions and comments about the quality of this book,
please contact us at CustomerService@Harlequin.com.

Harlequin Enterprises ULC
22 Adelaide St. West, 41st Floor
Toronto, Ontario M5H 4E3, Canada
www.Harlequin.com

Printed in U.S.A.

New York Times and *USA TODAY* bestselling author **Caridad Piñeiro** is a Jersey girl who just wants to write and is the author of nearly fifty novels and novellas. She loves romance novels, superheroes, TV and cooking. For more information on Caridad and her dark, sexy romantic suspense and paranormal romances, please visit www.caridad.com.

Books by Caridad Piñeiro

Harlequin Intrigue

South Beach Security

Lost in Little Havana

Cold Case Reopened
Trapping a Terrorist
Decoy Training

Visit the Author Profile page at Harlequin.com.

CAST OF CHARACTERS

Ramon Gonzalez, III (Trey)—Marine Trey Gonzalez serves Miami Beach as an undercover detective. The son of two well-known police officers, Trey has to deal with the legacy of his family and their agency, South Beach Security. Determined to solve the murder of his partner, Trey turns to his family's agency for help.

Roni Lopez—Undercover police detective Roni Lopez has known the Gonzalez family all her life. Best friend to Trey's sister, Mia, she's had a crush on Trey forever. When Trey asks her to help investigate his partner's murder, Roni hopes she can help him get justice for his partner...but she also hopes Trey can think of her as more than his little sister's annoying friend.

Mia and Carolina Gonzalez—Trey's younger sister, Mia, and cousin Carolina run a successful lifestyle and gossip blog and are invited to every important event in Miami. That lets "the twins" gather a lot of information about what is happening in Miami to help Trey with his current investigation.

Josefina (Sophie) and Robert Whitaker, Jr.—Trey's cousins are genius tech gurus who work at South Beach Security and help with various investigations.

Chapter One

Music pounded out of speakers while a DJ positioned on a stage above the crowded dance floor, like a high priest at the altar, orchestrated the electronic beats. Tourists dressed in bright tropical hues danced and gyrated beside top model wannabes and disinterested locals. Overhead lights and strobes bathed them in a wash of neon color.

The South Beach nightclub was lit but danger lurked beneath all that glitter and glamour.

Miami Beach Detective Trey Gonzalez stood at one side of the packed club, searching for the confidential informant who had called to say he had info that might be of interest. His partner, Doug Adams, had gone off on his own earlier to meet his own CI and hadn't returned. As Trey scanned the area, he caught sight of his sister Mia and cousin Carolina jockeying for spots at the bar. The two women had been born on the same day and were almost inseparable, which was why everyone teasingly called them the Twins. As they were two of Miami's top influencers, he wasn't surprised to see them there since they regularly covered the club scene for their popular lifestyle blog. But he was worried that they might get caught up in the nasty things going on at the club.

His phone vibrated in his pocket, dragging his attention from the Twins. When he had time, he'd have to warn his sister and cousin away from this location. He pulled out his phone. His CI was calling.

"*¿Donde estas*, Eddie?" he asked, wondering where the man was since Trey hadn't spotted him in the club.

"*Mano*, I can't show my face tonight," Eddie said in hushed tones, making it hard for Trey to hear over the almost deafening music.

To combat the noise, Trey hurried outside into a Miami night that was so steamy it was like he had walked into a sauna. "*¿Que pasa?*"

"There's too much going down at the club, Trey," his CI said nervously and slightly out of breath, as if he was running from something. Was it personal Eddie issues or something bigger that might be dangerous to the Twins and other innocent bystanders?

"*Caray*, Eddie. What's happening?" Trey said, worried. Plus, his partner would be wondering where he had gone since they might be missing some of the drug dealing that he and his partner were undercover to prevent.

In a rapid-fire burst of words, Eddie spilled his sketchy story. "Looking for me there. I know about the women in a shipping container on Terminal Island. Sending them overseas to a human trafficking ring. Soon."

Trey would normally turn over that kind of case to other detectives in his precinct, but before he did, he wanted to confirm Eddie's information for himself. If Eddie was right, those women might not have much time left before being sold into slavery.

"Are you sure, Eddie?" he asked, since his CI was being a little too squirrelly, which sometimes meant his info was less than reliable.

"I'm sure, Trey. This is not good, *mano*," Eddie said, his tone urgent and choppy, as if he was at a full-out run. A millisecond later, the call ended.

Trey stared at his cell phone, puzzled. He tried to call Eddie back, but he didn't answer.

Both annoyed and worried, Trey rushed back into the club to look for his partner.

MIAMI BEACH DETECTIVE Roni Lopez worked her way through the club, her walk one that any fashion model on a catwalk would envy. She was there to draw the attention of the man they suspected of having abducted a number of women in the South Beach area. Roni had only the barest information on the alleged kidnapper and a police sketch from a woman who had luckily managed to avoid a similar fate. The man might also be responsible for the disappearance days earlier of two college students.

As Roni neared the bar, she caught sight of her best friends, Mia and her cousin Carolina. They were dressed to the nines in dresses that had to be designer and Louboutins with their distinctive red soles. Mia's almost seal-black hair was cut short in a stylish bob while Carolina's hair hung in soft waves to her shoulders. Men scrambled around them, eager to buy them drinks, but her friends politely refused the offers.

She sauntered over for a quick hello and to warn them about the club—that it was a possible hunting ground for a kidnapper, although her friends were unlikely targets. As well-known influencers, their disappearance would bring too much attention. It was much easier to grab women who would not be missed as quickly, like sex workers. That was why she had been surprised to find that the college students had been taken while on a school trip. Their absence had been noted within 48 hours.

Roni slipped an arm around her friends' waists and dropped quick kisses on their cheeks. She wiped away a red lipstick stain she left behind on Mia's cheek.

Mia smiled and said, "*Hola, mi amiga.* What brings you here tonight?"

In a whisper so that only her friends could hear, she said, "Work, unfortunately."

"You and Trey. You just missed him," Carolina said and tossed her head toward the far side of the club.

Roni looked that way, but Trey was nowhere to be found.

"Disappointed?" Mia teased, well aware that Roni had once had a massive crush on her older brother. That crush had dimmed but not totally disappeared, given the way her heart had jumped at the mention of Trey's name. But he was Mia's brother as well as a fellow Miami Beach police detective and therefore definitely off-limits.

"Been there, done that," Roni lied and shot a quick look around again, searching for the handsome detective. She didn't see Trey, but she suddenly spied Trey's partner, Doug Adams, speaking to a man who looked way too much like the police sketch of her possible suspect. She was about to walk over when Doug's gaze locked with hers.

Doug's eyes widened in surprise, and he quickly leaned toward the other man to say something. The man looked her way, his blue eyes as flat as a shark's, rousing a chill in her center. Dangerous eyes. Maybe even the eyes of a kidnapper.

She took a step toward them, but they separated and raced off in different directions.

Roni muttered a curse under her breath and murmured a hasty goodbye to her friends. "Gotta run. Stay safe, okay."

"You, too," they said in unison as Roni hurried after the man with the cold dead eyes.

TREY SEARCHED THE club for his partner. If Eddie was right, women's lives were at stake, and they had to get moving to investigate what was happening on Terminal Island.

A second later, Doug dashed out of the back room, his head hunched down into his shoulders, like he was trying to hide from someone. Doug peered around the room, clearly uneasy. Concerned, Trey hustled over to him, but Doug jerked his head in the direction of the exit.

On the street, Doug continued to scan the area, but as they blended into the pedestrians strolling along Ocean Drive, his partner relaxed. Doug's earlier nervousness was out of character for the man he'd been working with for the last five years. Doug was normally laid-back even in the most difficult of situations.

"What's up, *mano*?" Trey asked, but his friend only shrugged and said, "Nothing, dude."

Trey scrutinized his partner, not satisfied by his curt reply. "You seem spooked."

"It's nothing, Trey," he insisted. "What did Eddie have to say?"

With each step that they got away from the club his partner's tension eased, so Trey left it alone and reported on his CI's information. "Eddie says there's something going down on Terminal Island. Women waiting to be trafficked."

At his words, Doug's shoulders tightened up again and Trey's gut warned him something was totally wrong with his partner.

Doug tossed him a nervous look. "Do you believe him?"

With a shrug, Trey said, "There's a reason they call him 'Eddie *la Rata*.'" Despite that, there had been an urgency in Eddie's voice that warned there was a lot of truth to his story.

"But when you see him, you'll still gave the rat a Benjamin for the info," Doug said, doubt obvious in his tone.

With another shrug, Trey said, "Have to keep the info flowing. Besides, it's a slow night. We might as well check it out."

"Might as well," Doug echoed, but Trey detected conflict in his partner. Apprehension snaked through his gut that Doug was keeping something from him.

When they reached the spot where earlier that night they had parked Trey's restored Camaro SS, they got in and Trey cruised down Ocean Drive. As he drove, Trey searched the nighttime crowds in front of the hotels and restaurants along the street and then skipped his gaze over to Lummus Park. He identified several of the locals he knew to be trouble, before shooting a quick glance at his partner, who had likewise been keeping track of the comings and goings along the strip.

Doug kept silent as Trey pulled off Ocean Drive and headed to the MacArthur Causeway and Terminal Island. The location was home to a number of cargo and yacht facilities as well as a coast guard station and the Fisher Island Ferry and according to Eddie, the shipping container with the women who would soon be sold into slavery.

Because there was regular traffic from the ferry and businesses on the island, Trey was a little doubtful about Eddie *la Rata*'s story. Even if it was true, it had to be a small-time operation if anyone hoped to keep their human trafficking secret. Too much activity was bound to draw attention. But if there was even one woman in trouble, Trey thought, it was worth investigating if they could stop the kind of misery awaiting her.

"If there is some truth to it, we'll have to call in our friends in Miami-Dade," he said. Terminal Island was under the jurisdiction of the Miami-Dade police and not his Miami Beach department.

"Makes you wonder if they don't already know about this and we're wrecking one of their investigations." Doug drummed his fingers along the edge of the closed window of the car.

"More reason to call and let them know we're visiting." It hit him again that Doug wasn't keen on checking out Eddie's story, but Trey wasn't about to be dissuaded. Too much was at stake.

He phoned one of their local contacts to give him

the heads-up and the man quickly said, "I think you're barking up the wrong tree, *chico*."

"Probably, but we didn't want to step on any toes. We'll let you know if we dig anything up," Trey replied and hung up after the man thanked him. The Miami-Dade detective also promised to call it into their dispatch center so others would be aware of their location.

They exited onto Terminal Island and Trey slowed the car to a crawl and shut off the headlights. He wanted to stay undetected in the more deserted parts of the island. Opening the windows, he listened for sounds of anything unusual. The humidity of the Miami night filled the car along with the odors of diesel fuel and rotting fish. In the distance, the whir of car tires from the causeway mingled with the slap of waves against boat hulls in the nearby marina.

Trey slowly maneuvered the car around the access road past a utility company's power plant. A number of shipping containers sat nearby in a fairly dark and less-traveled area. He parked the car and he and Doug exited the vehicle and made the rounds in and around the first few containers. Their shoes crunched on the gravel while the bright beams of their flashlights pierced the dark gloom around the hulking shapes.

Trey was vigilant for signs of anything out of the ordinary. He swiveled his head back and forth, peering into every nook and cranny, but there was nothing. *Nada.* Eddie's story was smelling fishier than the stink coming off the nearby waters.

All was quiet until they reached an area between the entrance to a cargo facility and a storage area for a marina on the island. Ahead of him Trey noticed a trio of shipping containers tucked into a far corner. The muffled sounds of voices and metal scraping on metal, the noise like nails on a chalkboard, drifted into the night from inside the container.

The hackles on the back of Trey's neck rose sharply. Despite the heat of the night, a chill clawed into his center and his heart jumped in his chest. *This is so not good.*

With a quick glance at Doug, Trey motioned for him to pull back, uneasy. His partner and he were likely outmanned and outgunned. Best to wait for backup. His partner took shelter behind a nearby storage shed and Trey met him there.

"Looks like Eddie was telling the truth," Doug said and peered from around the corner of the shed. The grate of metal doors shifting grew loud in the quiet of the night.

Trey likewise risked a look. The door on one of the shipping containers opened and the spill of light allowed a glimpse of at least one man sitting at a table inside as another stepped out.

"We need to call Miami-Dade for backup," Trey said, and Doug nodded.

But then a piercing woman's scream and the loud sound of a slap escaped through the open door before the man could close it. Doug charged ahead, fully exposed in the bright moonlight. The man who had exited the container spotted him, drew his weapon and fired. Round after round spit from his submachine gun and chased Doug as he raced for protection.

Trey shot at the man, trying to provide cover for Doug, drawing the man's fire in his direction. Sparks flew as the bullets hit the shed, driving him back. But as the shooting turned back toward Doug, he peered out.

Two other men raced out of the container, guns drawn. They opened fire on Doug's position. His partner stumbled and fell back.

Trey cursed, grabbed his cell phone and quickly phoned for backup. "Officer down. Officer down," he said and spit out a location to the dispatcher.

Shadows raced out from around the shipping container, armed men heading toward his partner. Too many. A cold sweat erupted across Trey's body. He tightened his grip on his weapon and sucked in a rough breath, preparing himself.

He couldn't wait for backup if he was going to save Doug.

"Police! Drop your weapons!" he shouted, well aware they wouldn't comply. As more gunshots rang out, he rushed forward, shooting at the men to draw their attention. His heart pounded in his chest as fear and adrenaline raced through his veins.

The first bullet grazed him high on the thigh. He ignored the bite of pain and pushed forward, shooting as he sped toward his partner. His Glock jumped in his hand, the muzzle flash bright in the dark night. The metallic smell of his blood and sulfury gunpowder filled his nostrils while the sharp retort of his weapon echoed in his ears.

Two men dropped as his shots struck home. Before he could take cover, another gunshot caught him high on the shoulder. It jerked him back for a moment and slowed his race to his partner.

One of the attackers rushed to where Trey had seen Doug fall. One, two, three shots rang out. The sound reverberated against the metal of the containers.

Trey screamed in anguish, fired and loaded a new magazine, but the man was already running back toward his compatriots and shouting out instructions for them to clear out. Mindlessly Trey dashed toward his partner. Motion came from behind a container. He turned to confront the man and a bullet tore across his ribs. It drove him to his knees, but not before he got off a shot and took down his attacker.

Eyesight failing, he fell forward, but somehow garnered the strength to crawl toward his partner, who sat immobile against the wall of a storage container. Doug's eyes were wide-open and staring at the night sky. Blossoms of red spread across his chest and midsection.

Trey pulled Doug into his arms and cradled him close. The wet of his tears mingled with blood and sweat. His. Doug's. Vision fading, Trey silently pleaded for his partner's life. Prayed for his own as a chill settled into his midsection and slowly spread.

Dios, por favor, he thought, peering at a bright Miami moon that dimmed as he grew faint from blood loss. But then the sounds of sirens screeched into the night.

Trey sucked in a rough breath, fighting to hold on. Help was on its way. Maybe it wasn't too late. *Hold on just a little longer.* Maybe then he'd be able to ask his partner why he'd raced out into almost certain death. Had it been the woman's scream or something else?

With cold settling into his gut, Trey tightened his

arms around his partner as if by doing so he could keep him in this world. Maybe then he'd know the answer to the questions that chased him into unconsciousness.

Chapter Two

Trey woke to a world of hurt.

Pain came at him from all sides, but he drove it out of his consciousness and focused on other things. The pinch and pull of the IV in his arm. The slight nip in the room and rough hospital sheets beneath his body. The warm gentle touch of a hand. His mother's hand, he knew, without even opening his eyes. He grabbed hold tight.

"Mi'jo," she said, her tones soft and laced with a different kind of pain.

He cracked his eyes open and met his mother's worried gaze. But he could see in her eyes something more. Fear. "Doug?"

"I'm sorry, *mi'jo.*"

Trey sucked in a breath to fight back the tears but grimaced as another wave of pain buffeted his body.

"Easy, Trey," he heard another voice say and glanced toward the door where his father stood. Deep lines etched his forehead and bracketed his mouth. Dark smudges beneath his eyes, like charcoal smoothed across paper, made his skin sickly pale.

His father took a spot beside his mother, hand resting on her shoulder. As Trey gazed at them, it occurred to him that his parents seemed to have aged decades since the last time he'd seen them barely a week earlier. Which made him wonder how long he'd been out of it since he'd been shot.

"What day is it?" he asked, voice rusty from disuse and the tubes they had likely shoved down his throat.

"Sunday," his mother said.

He and his partner Doug had been investigating a lead on Friday night when the barrage of bullets had cut them down. Which meant Doug had been dead for two days.

"He shouldn't have run out. I should have stopped him," he said as guilt erupted again at the thought of Doug's young wife and the two toddlers who would never know their father.

"Then it might have been you that's dead, *mi'jo*," his father said with none of his mother's tenderness, but the worry and love were still there. Along with something else that he knew was coming: his father's hope that Trey would leave the police department and join the family business.

"*Por favor, papi.* Not now," he said and closed his eyes, his strength quickly fading, drained by both his emotions and injuries.

As his mother's soft touch came against his hand once more, he centered on that loving caress and let himself slip away so he could heal. The faster he healed, the faster he could find out why his partner hadn't waited for backup. Find out who had murdered Doug.

RONI STOOD BEHIND the Twins as they showered Trey with hugs and kisses.

"*Hermanito*, you had us so worried," Mia said and

hugged her older brother. Carolina playfully elbowed Mia out of the way to drop a quick kiss on her cousin's cheek. "Totally worried," Carolina said.

Trey glanced her way and offered a pained and slightly weak smile, but his color was good and he'd managed to sit upright in bed without any help. "Thank you all for coming by, but I'll be fine," he said, his voice raspy.

If you could consider being shot in three different places fine, Roni thought, but he seemed stronger than after his operation two days earlier. After losing her suspect when he'd raced out of the club, she'd headed to another bar in the hopes of finding him, but she'd had no luck. She had returned to the bar to make sure her friends were fine. That was when Trey's parents had called Mia to tell her about the shooting.

At that moment, her heart had stopped in her chest and the only thing she could think was, *Not Trey*.

"You better be fine, Gonzalez," Roni said, trying to keep her tone upbeat. Two nights ago, when she'd driven the Twins to the hospital, it had been too scary to see him unconscious and in pain.

Trey nodded and said, "I will be. Bet on it."

Knowing Trey, she wouldn't bet against him. And knowing Trey, he'd be determined to find out who had murdered his partner. She was just as determined to find the suspect who had been talking to Doug that night and discover what had been his relationship to Trey's partner. Worry niggled in her gut that it hadn't been anything aboveboard.

Shooting a glance at her watch, she said, "I should get going. My partner is probably wondering where I am this morning."

"Thanks for coming," Trey said and jerked his chin up in a bro-kind of goodbye. No hugs and kisses for her and disappointment flared before she tamped it down.

"Sure. See you." She was tempted for a moment, a too-brief moment, to go over and give him a hug or a kiss. But she was afraid it might reveal too much, especially with the Twins watching. They were well aware of her crush and would be only too happy to play matchmaker.

She hurried from the room, eager to return to the station house and brief her new partner on what she'd seen the night of Trey's shooting. Her partner had been undercover at a different club, keeping an eye on things there. They hadn't had a chance to really chat since they'd been caught up with processing the human trafficking victims and reviewing the initial evidence from the shooting as well as coordinating with Miami-Dade on the case.

Traffic was light on the way from the hospital to Miami Beach. Her partner was at his desk when she entered, but she had barely taken a few steps into the station house when her captain called out to her.

"Detective Lopez, I need you ASAP," he said from the door of his office.

She shot a quick look at her partner, sitting at his desk, but he only gave her a "who knows" shrug.

But when she entered, she found two of the department's internal affairs detectives standing to one side of her captain's office.

"Detective Lopez," the first IAD detective said. Ramirez was an older, former football player whose size was imposing, but who was also starting to spread around the middle.

His sidekick, Detective Anderson, was years younger, with blond surfer boy looks and a lean muscular body. Anderson tilted his head up in greeting as her captain gestured in the direction of the chair in front of his desk. Once she sat, he closed the door behind her.

"Captain Rogers?" she asked, but he said nothing, just settled into his chair and glared at the IAD men. His face was set in harsh lines, his brown skin taut against the sharp line of his jaw. Mahogany brown eyes glittered with anger and his hands were folded over his midsection, fingers laced together tightly.

"We understand that you and Detective Gonzalez are quite friendly," Ramirez said, and she didn't fail to miss the insinuation in his tone.

"His sister and cousin are my best friends, and our families are close. We've basically grown up together," she said to clear up any misconceptions about the nature of their relationship.

Ramirez and Anderson shared a look that caused a frisson of fear to race down Roni's spine and worry tightened her gut into a knot.

"How well do you know Detective Gonzalez?" Anderson said.

"As I said, we've grown up together," she said and risked a quick glance at her captain, whose position and demeanor had only gotten more agitated, matching her own growing disquiet.

"What's this about?" Roni asked, cutting to the chase.

The two IAD detectives glanced at each other once more before Ramirez said, "We have reason to believe that Detective Adams was involved in something that might be responsible for what happened two nights ago."

The image of Doug speaking with her possible suspect flashed through her brain.

"Detective?" Anderson said, clearly picking up on her unease.

"I don't believe it could be something criminal," she said, even as doubt tangled with the worry in her gut.

Ramirez had been holding a manila folder and at her response, he opened it, yanked out some papers and handed them to her. "You understand that as soon as an officer is murdered under certain circumstances, we have to review every aspect of their cases and private lives as necessary."

Roni scrutinized what appeared to be printouts from Doug's bank accounts. There were two large deposits into the accounts just a couple of days before the shooting. Just too much coincidence and way too condemning. She shook her head and said, "There has to be a reasonable explanation for this. This has to be a mistake."

"No mistake, Lopez. Adams was being paid off, for what we don't know, but we intend to find out. We want you to help us," Anderson said, his tone brusque.

Help them prove that Trey's partner was dirty? That whatever he was doing was responsible for not only his death, but Trey's shooting? Did they think Trey was also dirty?

"Detective?" Ramirez pressed, leaning his big body toward her in challenge.

Despite the papers she was staring at, it was still hard

for her to believe that Trey's partner had done anything illegal. There had to be a reasonable explanation for the money in the bank accounts. Something that would explain the shooting. Anything that she could use to make sense of why Doug Adams had been talking to the man who might be responsible for the disappearance of her two missing college students and possibly other women.

"Do you think Trey…Detective Gonzalez…was aware of what his partner was doing?" she said and handed the papers back to the IAD detectives.

"We don't have any evidence at this time that would suggest that," Ramirez said as he slipped the printouts back into his folder.

"There isn't any evidence because Trey isn't dirty and I can't believe Doug was either," Roni insisted, loyal to a man who was like family, and his partner. A man she cared about more than she should.

Anderson shook his head, as if in disbelief. "Put up or shut up, Lopez. If we're wrong, prove it, but if we're not…"

She didn't want to think about what would happen if they weren't wrong. How it would impact Trey, but more importantly, Doug's wife and the two young children he had left behind.

But the seeds of doubt had been sown about Trey's partner. And if all of that was tied to her own missing persons case, all the more reason to assist IAD as much as she might hate the thought. Or as much as Trey might see it as a betrayal.

"Captain," she said, to draw the other man's attention. He swiveled in his chair and turned his dark gaze on her, conflicting emotions evident there. "Are you on board with me assisting in this investigation?"

He laid his intertwined hands on his desk and bounced them up and down. "I am. We need to know what really happened that night. And as far as I'm concerned, we need to clear our officer's name because I do not believe Adams was involved in anything criminal."

With a nod, Roni returned her attention to the two IAD detectives. "What do you want me to do?"

"YOU'RE CRAZY, *HERMANITO*. You're in no shape to go to the funeral today," his younger sister Mia said as Trey swung his legs over the edge of the bed.

"For sure, Trey," echoed his cousin Carolina, who shot a worried look at Mia. Today the Twins were both dressed in staid black dresses, so different from their usual flamboyant colors and outfits.

"*Chicas*, I'm fine," he said, even though his head spun from the simplest of movements and little beads of sweat broke out across his top lip.

A second later his brother Ricardo hurried in, Trey's dress uniform draped across his arm. As his younger brother peered at Trey, he shook his head. *"Loco, completamente loco."*

"Give it a rest and help me, Ricky," he complained and held out his hand for the uniform.

Ricky, Mia and Carolina shared a concerned glance, but then Ricky shrugged and said, "You can't stop crazy. I'll help him. We'll see you later."

The Twins dropped quick kisses on Trey's cheek and hurried out of the room to let Trey dress.

Every movement brought renewed pain, even with

his brother Ricky helping him into his clothes the way a mother would assist a clumsy toddler. By the time they were done, a chill sweat covered his body, and his muscles trembled. Despite his best intentions, Trey wasn't sure he could even stand, but then his father and grandfather walked in, likewise outfitted in their old dress uniforms. Right behind them came Roni Lopez, surprising him, but the Twins had probably told her of his intent to attend Doug's funeral. Like the men, she was in her dress uniform, her hat tucked under her arm. She rolled in a wheelchair and his mind rebelled at the thought of being pushed around like a baby.

He was about to protest when she said, "Save yourself for the funeral, Gonzalez. It won't do anyone any good if you face plant before you even get there."

He met her hazel-eyed gaze and was struck by how beautiful she was. Even in cop clothes. And bossy, he realized as she motioned to the chair and said, "Move it. We don't have all day."

Trey skipped a glance at his father and grandfather, who only shrugged. Their faces were set in serious lines, but as he stood and wavered, worry swept over their features. His brother Ricky quickly offered his arm for support as Trey dropped heavily into the wheelchair.

"We're off," Roni said and laid a reassuring hand on his shoulder before she wheeled him from the room.

Trey reached up and smoothed his hand over hers, drawing comfort from that gentle touch, yet bracing himself for what was going to be a difficult day. Grateful for the support of his family and Roni.

Roni. She'd intrigued him forever, even as an awkward and too-shy teen. She'd always hung out with the

Twins, so much so he had jokingly said they should be called the Triplets. Always there, but always more circumspect than his flamboyant sister and cousin.

As she'd grown up before his eyes, it had been ever harder not to notice the dangerous Cuban curves that had erupted on her slender body. And her face. Almost gamine, but beautifully different. Her eyes, hazel shot through with gold and filled with intelligence and caring.

He risked a glance at her and that compelling gaze melded with his, providing solace along with the touch of her hand on his shoulder once more. It was as if to say, "You can do it," and he would.

He had to say goodbye to the partner he had failed and comfort the family left behind by his death.

After, he would find out who had done this and mete out justice for Doug.

Chapter Three

Police officers, family members, politicians and citizens intent on honoring a fallen hero jammed the church for the funeral and spilled out into the gardens in front of the bayfront cathedral dedicated to Cuba's patron saint. The police officers were from all over the state and beyond, their dress uniforms a sea of different blues and blacks in the crowd.

As they entered the church, Trey leaned heavily on the cane his grandfather had insisted he take when Trey had balked at using the wheelchair. Trey hadn't argued with him because he never won an argument with his grandfather. He might be 87, but the founder of South Beach Security remained formidable.

Trey was grateful for the cane since every step brought agony in each of the spots where he'd been shot. His leg burned with the movement and the pull of stitches along his ribcage and shoulder warned him not to exert himself, no matter how much he wanted to get to Doug's family to offer his condolences.

When he stumbled at one point, Roni was at his side, providing support, and he offered her a grateful look.

At the front of the church, Roni peeled away to sit

in a row with other officers from their precinct. Trey stopped in front of the pew holding Doug's young wife, children and other family members. Doug's wife rose and reached for him across the top of the wooden pew.

"Trey," she whispered and buried her head against his chest.

He wrapped his arm around her, leaned his head toward hers, and whispered, "I'm so, so sorry, Linda."

She nodded and snared his gaze, her eyes redrimmed from crying and shimmering with fresh tears. "Promise me you'll get whoever did this."

"I promise," he whispered and tightened his hold on her.

A gentle touch came at his arm, and he met his father's troubled gaze.

"It's time, *mi' jo*," he said, and Trey peered toward the entrance to the church. Beyond the doors, a cadre of fellow officers waited beside the coffin draped with an American flag. Behind them, hundreds of police officers were lined up, hoping to enter the church and pay their last respects.

With a nod and his father's support, he tottered to the pew packed with Gonzalez family members and took a seat, his body shaky from his physical exertions; his emotions raw as the funeral procession began.

How had this happened? As he'd lain in the hospital bed the last four days, counting the tiles in the ceiling, he'd asked himself that multiple times. Asked himself how they hadn't seen the danger that night. Although his body sat in the church for the funeral, his mind drifted back to the night of the shooting, trying to make sense of all that had happened. Doug's weirdness and inexplicable charge toward the armed man. The phone call from Eddie that had set the whole night in motion.

Eddie who had yet to respond to any of the calls he'd made in the two days since waking up after his surgery.

Had something happened to Eddie as well?

He was so lost in his thoughts that he didn't realize Mass was over until the others in his pew rose as the coffin started its trip down the aisle. Slowly he stood, leaning heavily on the cane and the top edge of the pew. Sweat ran down the back of his neck and his legs trembled, but he stayed upright until the coffin and Doug's family left the church.

Only then did he plop onto the pew and wipe sweat from his forehead. Gathering his strength, he waited as the crowds exited the building. He was about to rise when two men came to stand before his pew. They were dressed in dark wrinkled suits and as he looked up, he recognized them immediately. Anger erupted, but he tamed it, telling himself that the IAD detectives were only there to pay their last respects.

"Detective Gonzalez. Our condolences on the loss of your partner," the older man said, hands clasped before him in a familiar cop pose. But there was something in his gaze that Trey didn't like.

"*Gracias*, Detective Ramirez. Is that the only reason you're here?" Trey said, and his father laid a hand on his shoulder in warning.

"We understand it's a bad time," said the other man.

"That's an understatement, Detective Anderson," Trey replied, disgust coloring his words despite the very real compassion in the second detective's voice.

"When you're up to it, please give us a call." Detective Ramirez reached into his pocket and extracted a business card. Trey took it without hesitation because he had nothing to fear from the two internal affairs officers.

Despite that, Trey challenged them. "But don't wait too long, *verdad*?"

"The sooner the better, Gonzalez. We want to find out what happened to your partner as much as you do," Ramirez responded, and before Trey could say anything else, the two men walked out, following the last of the mourners from the church. As they did so, the mournful sounds of bagpipes filtered in.

As Trey rose, Roni slipped from her pew and stood in front of him. He met her gaze and it hit him. "You knew about this, didn't you?"

Roni tilted her chin up at a defiant angle. "There were rumors around the precinct about an IAD investigation, but no one thinks you're dirty."

It was also impossible to miss what she wasn't saying— "But not Doug."

With a shrug, she said, "I'm not sure, but if you're willing, I'm here to help."

He dipped his head and skipped his gaze over her beautiful features. As his gaze locked with hers, he detected a maelstrom of emotions beneath her calm exterior. "Why, Roni?"

With another shrug, she said, "You're *familia*, Trey. Family helps family."

She didn't wait for his reply before turning on her heel and heading down the aisle of the church. As he watched her go, his father squeezed his shoulder and leaned into him, saying, "It's going to be okay, *mi'jo*. We'll help you get to the bottom of this."

Trey normally got defensive when his father offered his helpful and sometimes unwanted advice, but this was one time he wasn't going to argue with him or refuse his help. He'd do anything to find out the truth behind his partner's death. *"Gracias, papi."*

Trey leaned heavily on the cane as he slowly walked down the aisle and to their car for the long, sad trip to the cemetery. His mind bounced from one thing to another as he thought about the visit from Internal Affairs, his own doubts about his partner's actions that night and Roni. So many unknowns to deal with and he hoped he'd be up to the challenge both physically and emotionally.

A FEW DAYS later Roni was at her desk when the wave of whispers rushing across the station like a tsunami warned her something was up. She glanced toward the entrance to find Trey walking in slowly. His color was better than it had been at the funeral, his tanned skin free of the unhealthy hospital pallor. His full lips were locked tight, and as a lock of his almost black hair tumbled onto his forehead, he brushed it back in obvious irritation.

Her stomach did a little jump as he shot her an abrupt look. But then he was moving away into one of the interrogation rooms, and seconds later the two internal affairs detectives followed him in.

When the IAD detectives had first reached out to her she had been hard-pressed to believe what they'd told her about Trey's partner. Plus, it worried her that Trey had possibly missed what was going on with Adams. He had been involved in law enforcement for too long to miss something like that.

As the third Gonzalez to serve in the Miami Beach PD, he was like law enforcement royalty. In the Cuban American community, the Gonzalez family and the private security and investigative agency they ran, South Beach Security, were local legends.

In the days since that first meeting with IAD, she'd been unable to find out anything else about Doug's activities and had reported that to the two detectives. But she couldn't deny that there had been something off with Trey's partner when she'd spotted him in the back room of the club that night. Doug had seemed pretty spooked that she'd seen him. She intended to discuss it with Trey once he was done with IAD. She had actually wanted to mention it to him earlier, but with his recovery and the funeral she had decided it was best to wait for a better time.

Turning her attention to her current case, she reviewed the details of where the two students had gone missing and compared that to the testimony of the women who had been held captive in the shipping containers that Trey and Doug had discovered just barely a week earlier. She also compared it to the story that their sole earlier witness had provided. Their stories were similar, but not the same. The two Terminal Island women, both sex workers who generally covered the Ocean Drive area, had gone to one of the local clubs and met an interesting man who had invited them to a private party at one of the high-end South Beach hotels. The party had started out fine, but neither woman was able to remember how their night had ended, only that they had woken up blindfolded and tied up at another location. There they had been sexually assaulted over the course of the next few days before losing consciousness and waking in the shipping containers. Both women's recollections of the man who had taken them to the party had been hazy but fit a general description of the man she had briefly seen with Doug.

Their sole earlier witness had likewise assisted in creating a sketch that matched that of the two sex workers and she had also been invited to a party. But in her case, she recalled going to a fancy private home where she thought she'd been roofied. Somehow, she'd managed to stumble out of that home, run off and hide before being able to call a friend in the morning to come to get her. Unfortunately, neither she nor the friend had been able to pinpoint the location of that home.

But the suspect in both cases seemed to be the same man. That made her wonder at the connection between Doug and the man and whether that had had anything to do with Doug's murder.

The rough slam of a door and rattle of glass in the frame made her peer in the direction of the interrogation room.

Trey stormed out, limping slightly as he sped away, his features set in fierce lines, tension radiating from every line in his body. Seconds later, the two internal affairs detectives walked out, looking not much happier than Trey. Ramirez tapped a file against his thigh while Anderson glared at Trey's retreating back.

When Ramirez noticed her looking their way, he called out, "What are you eyeballing, Lopez?"

She wanted to say, "Two *idiotas*," but let her silence speak for itself. It had been agreed that no one would be aware that she was helping IAD so she had a role to play to keep that secret.

She dragged her attention back to her case file, but before she could get into her analysis too deeply, her cell phone chirped with a text message.

Trey. Still want to help?

She peeked around to see who might be watching. It was clear, so she texted, I'm yours. Then she winced at how flirty that sounded. There was just too much going on for her to be thinking of him in that way. She had to focus on finding out what had really happened with his partner and her missing college students.

But that didn't make it any easier to control her attraction to the sexy detective.

After a bit of a delay, which had her wondering what he was thinking about her response, Trey texted, Barnacle Bill's. Way in the back behind the pool tables.

Barnacle Bill's was a favorite hangout for local law enforcement and rumored to have been around since the wild heyday of the Magic City when Julia Tuttle had convinced Flagler to bring his Florida East Coast Railway to the area.

With another quick glance around to make sure no one was watching, she texted back, On my way.

She unlocked her drawer, grabbed her service pistol and tucked it into her shoulder holster. Slipping on a lightweight blazer to hide her weapon, she told her partner, "Taking a break, Heath. I'll be at Barnacle Bill's if you need me."

"You got it, Roni," her partner replied with a mock salute.

She hurried out of the station, through the small plaza in front of the building and across the street to Barnacle Bill's.

At the door, she ran her hand over the well-worn belly of a wooden pelican by the entrance, a good luck ritual that had developed over the decades. The pelican's belly had been worn smooth to a golden hue from the many touches. Grabbing hold of the brass handles shaped like rope, she yanked open the heavy wooden door and stepped into the dark interior of the bar.

The decor inside matched the kitschy exterior with lots of dark wood and ropes, seashells and nautical paintings as well as sport-fishing trophies on various walls. The mustiness from Miami humidity lingered, mixed with the yeasty aroma of beer and sweet fried onions.

She jerked her head in greeting at the bartender wiping down the bar and pushed through the eating area and past the pool tables to the more secluded booths in the back. She spotted Trey immediately. He rose to greet her as she neared, dropped a quick, very fraternal peck on her cheek and motioned to one of the waitresses to come over.

"What can I get you, sweetie?" the older woman said as she pulled out a pad and pen. A helmet of pure white hair wreathed a face free of wrinkles for someone her age.

"Seltzer with lemon, please," she said and eased into the booth opposite Trey.

"Thanks for coming," he said and shifted his own glass back and forth across the surface of the table.

"Like I said before, *familia*." *Liar*, the little voice in her head screamed, but she strangled it back.

He narrowed his gaze, examined her and seemingly satisfied by her lie, he said, "*Gracias*. I wish those two IAD idiots treated their fellow officers like family instead of criminals. They think Doug was dirty. That he was going to warn the men in the containers when he was shot."

"Do *you* think that?" she asked and watched his features for any telltale signs.

Trey hesitated, maybe a moment too long, and before he could answer, the waitress brought over her drink.

"Thanks," she said and when the woman had left, she pressed Trey. "Well?"

Trey wagged his head and batted the glass back and forth again on a surface made slick from the sweat off the glass. "I've replayed those moments over and over. I don't know why Doug rushed ahead. A woman had screamed. We heard a slap like she was being beaten. Maybe that's why. Maybe he thought she was in immediate danger."

She stared at him over the rim of her glass before taking a sip. "But maybe it was for some other reason."

Another awkward hesitation came before Trey finally said, "I'd rather not think that about a man who was a friend and saved my ass more than once. A man whose home was like *my home* and whose kids call me Uncle Trey."

Roni understood his upset because it not only meant his partner was dirty, it also meant Trey had possibly been a very poor judge of character. "Why does IAD think Doug is dirty?" she asked, even though she knew. She had to keep up the ruse so he wouldn't know she was working with them. That she was betraying him.

He hesitated and that infinitesimally small pause kindled worry in her gut that he didn't trust her.

"They have copies of Doug's bank accounts. Someone put money there."

His admission to that fact quickly smothered her spark of concern.

"If you don't believe it—"

"I don't," he said with a shake of his head, his voice rising. A lock of dark hair fell forward and he brushed it back, irritated, and plowed on. "I know who can help us find out."

"Sophie and Rob," she said without hesitation. His Whitaker cousins were computer experts and ethical hackers who often worked on cases with the family's business, South Beach Security. That he would think to use his family's resources showed how worried he was about the IAD accusations. For as long as she could remember, Trey had wanted distance from his family's business and resisted familial pressure to join the agency.

"*Sí*, Sophie and Rob," he said, then picked up his glass and took a long chug of the liquid, possibly upset with having to use SBS resources.

While she didn't want to add to his worry, it was as good a time as any to tell him about what she had seen. "Doug was with someone at the club that night."

Trey nodded, not surprised. "He went to see a CI."

Roni shook her head. "It didn't seem like that kind

of talk. And there was something…weird about Doug. He was really antsy, especially when he realized I'd seen him. He broke it off then and hurried away. So did the other man."

Trey leaned back and sucked in a rough breath. "Did you recognize the man?"

With a lift of her shoulders, she said, "Maybe. I'm working on a missing persons case. Two college students who never returned to their hotel. We have a witness to an earlier attempted kidnapping, and she helped with a police sketch. The man Doug met looked like that sketch."

She reached out and laid a hand over his as he held his glass. "The two women you found were sex workers who had similar experiences. They were pretty sure that my suspect was the man who took them to private parties where they were roofied. There's just too much coincidence for all these cases not to be connected."

"I agree that the cases are probably related. And my CI Eddie, who tipped us off that night, is missing. I haven't heard from him in a week," Trey admitted with worry.

"I can issue a BOLO for him if you want since I assume you're on leave for now."

"I am on medical leave for at least another week and desk duty after that, but I'm not going to wait to investigate."

"I get it. I'll get a BOLO out for Eddie. He's obviously important to the investigation."

She sipped her seltzer again as Trey narrowed his gaze and said, "Are you sure about what you saw,

Roni? About the connections and the suspect in all three cases?"

Roni nodded. "I am. I was undercover at the club that night because it was one of the locations where my witness had been before her attempted kidnapping. And all the women seem to have the same general impression of the man."

With a quick dip of his head, Trey said, "I'd appreciate that BOLO, Roni. And anything else you can help with." He rose, tossed some bills on the table and held his hand out for her. She hesitated, but then slipped her hand into his and tried to ignore the heat that shot up her arm and ignited a blush along her cheeks.

"Anytime, Trey," she said and dragged her hand from his, earning a knowing smile from Trey that said he might be aware of what his touch had done to her.

They walked out of the bar together but parted on the sidewalk. Trey's Camaro SS was a few cars down from the entrance and she was headed back to the police station. She stepped into the street and tires burning rubber squealed angrily. The sound snared her attention as a car barreled toward her, but she froze at the sight of the driver behind the wheel.

The man from the club?

Strong hands jerked her back to safety and against a rock-hard chest as the car flew by and into the intersection, narrowly avoiding a collision with two other cars before speeding away.

Trey's powerful arms wrapped around her and held her steady in the protective gap between two parked cars. Her body trembled as adrenaline poured through her, igniting her nerve endings.

"Are you okay?" Trey whispered against her ear. His warm, fresh breath spilled against the side of her face, and his reassuring squeeze calmed her.

"I'm okay." She turned in his embrace to meet his concerned gaze and cupped his cheek. *"Gracias."*

"Idiot kids racing," he said and shook his head.

Only Roni was certain it hadn't been an idiot kid. "It was intentional, Trey. I think the driver was the man Doug met that night."

"Are you sure?" he pressed, and she understood why. If she was right, then maybe Doug was as dirty as IAD thought.

"It happened so fast, but… I'm pretty sure." She was also sure of one other thing. If it was her suspect, he wasn't going to give up until she was dead.

"WHAT DO YOU mean you missed her? I told you exactly where she would be," he said, stomping to the door of his office and slamming the door shut.

"You didn't mention she'd have someone with her. He pulled her out of the way, and I was going too fast to get off a shot," the other man replied.

"Fool. Did she see your face?" he asked, worried that there would be another loose end he'd have to tie up before they were able to get things under control.

A hesitant pause came across the line before the other man said, "No. She didn't."

Except he knew Lopez had already seen his man the other night at the club. If she could track down her suspect, it might lead her straight to him.

"Lie low. No more girls until I say so," he said.

"Boss isn't going to be happy about that."

"Tell the boss that if he wants to keep on doing business, he better watch what I say," he said and ended the call.

But as he did so, he knew Lopez and Gonzalez weren't going to leave this alone.

Lopez had already called IAD to tell them about the incident and confirm her suspicions about the driver.

And Gonzalez was dead set on finding out who had killed his partner.

Dead being the operative word.

The business was too profitable to let Lopez and Gonzalez close it down.

If his partners couldn't take care of the two cops, he would have to step in and do it himself.

Chapter Four

They had gone back into Barnacle Bill's after the attempt on her life because she had been too shaken to return to the precinct, and Trey had been worried that it wasn't safe for her there. But she had sneaked away into the bathroom to call IAD and report about the attempt and who had behind the wheel.

The heat of the coffee helped chase away the chill that had erupted in her body at the thought that someone had tried to kill her.

"Did anyone know that you were meeting me?" Trey asked and sipped his own coffee.

Roni shook her head. "I told Heath that I was heading here."

Tony eyeballed her intently. "Heath Williams? He's your partner now?"

She nodded. "Bill Shea retired a couple of months ago and they teamed me up with Heath. He came over from the Vice Division about two weeks ago. Why?"

Trey shrugged strong, impossibly broad shoulders. "I never heard anything bad about him, but... Doug and I had to do an operation with him once. Rubbed me the wrong way."

"Doug and Heath knew each other?" Roni asked, not liking where this might be going. Heath was privy to some, but not all, of the information she'd shared with Trey about Doug's actions that night. Had Heath also seen or talked to Doug that night? Was there more to that relationship than Heath had let on?

"They did, but I don't know how well. The operation didn't last for long," Trey said, but she could see that he was as troubled as she by the coincidence. Before she could say anything, he said, "I think it makes sense right now to give Heath as little information as possible about what we're doing."

She did a slow nod. "I agree. But he'll wonder what I'm up to if I'm not working with him on this case."

"This case being the reason Doug is dead and someone just tried to kill you," Trey pointed out, one dark brow arching upward.

"I'm not even sure how much he knows about the missing students. He's only just come on board this case in the last week," Roni countered although there was too much coincidence to ignore.

Trey hesitated, but then plowed on. "I know how hard it is to imagine Heath is dirty. Believe me, it's as hard for me to believe it about Doug."

Roni picked up her mug, hands still slightly unsteady as she took a sip. When she set the cup down, she said, "I'll mind what I say to him and what evidence he gets to see, but I don't know how long I can do that before he gets suspicious."

TREY WANTED TO tell her that they didn't have much time. One officer had already been murdered, and he

was sure that whoever had just tried to take out Roni
wasn't going to stop until she was dead as well. Probably sooner rather than later.

"I think it makes sense for you to ask for a few days
off so we can work on this together," he said, but kept
to himself, *And so I can keep you safe*.

While he hadn't said it, Roni understood. That was
clear, but he sensed there was something else going on
with her. "Is there something you're not telling me?"

Color blossomed across her cheeks and her hands
shook against the coffee mug, rattling it against the
tabletop. "N-n-no," she said, but he'd known her too
long not to see the lie.

He reached out and laid his hands on hers. They
trembled beneath his as he said, "Whatever it is, you
can tell me."

How I wish I could, Roni thought. But even though Trey
wasn't the focus of the IAD investigation, it wouldn't
take much for IAD to veer to Trey's direction. She
couldn't let that happen, and she couldn't fail Doug
and his family either. She'd hardly reported on anything
to IAD other than what had just happened, but if Trey
found out that she had agreed to work with them, he'd
never trust her again.

"We need to get to work on this ASAP," she said and
pushed on, slipping free of his grasp to count off each
item on her fingers. "First thing, find out how the money
got in Doug's accounts. Second, track down the suspect
at the club—"

"And who you think tried to run you down. Add finding Eddie *la Rata* to the list," he said, and she nodded.

"I'll head back to the precinct and ask Captain Rogers for a few personal days. Then I'll round up anything I think may be useful for us to review," she said.

Trey nodded. "First stop will be Sophie and Rob. If anyone can find out how the money got there, they can."

Roni couldn't argue that his Whitaker cousins were the kind of ethical hackers who could find out what had happened, but she was once again surprised he was reaching out to anyone associated with his family's South Beach Security. That he was using them now spoke volumes about his concerns over the case.

"I'll meet you there," she said and rose from the table, but he reached out and laid a hand on her arm.

"I'm going to stick to you like white on rice, Roni."

The thought of that sent her brain and body into overdrive, which was insane considering the situation they were in. But that's what Trey did to her. He took the logical, responsible, by-the-book Roni and made her want things that were impossible.

"I can take care of myself," she said and strode away from him, but he was immediately at her side, a possessive hand at the small of her back.

He leaned down and whispered in her ear, "White on rice."

She didn't continue to argue with him. There was too much to be done and too much at stake. The missing college students. Doug's reputation and his family. Possibly Trey's reputation. Her safety. But as a cop her safety was regularly on the line, which was why she'd put it last.

It took only a couple of minutes to leave Barnacle Bill's and reach the station house. She pushed through the doors while Trey waited in the plaza in front of the building. The fewer people who knew about their working together the better.

She marched to Captain Rogers's office. He was making a call and seemed a little surprised to see her there but motioned for her to wait for him. He hung up less than a minute later, rose and invited her to enter. Once she did, she closed the door and stood in front of his desk, uneasy about what she was about to ask.

"Detective Lopez. What can I do for you?"

She rocked back and forth on her low-heeled shoes and rushed ahead with her request. "I know this is probably the worst time to ask for this, what with a new partner, the investigation and everything, but I need to take a few days off."

His dark gaze narrowed to a sharp point, skewering her with its intensity. "You're right that this is the worst possible time, Detective. May I ask why?"

"It's… I'd rather not say, sir," she said, unable to lie to her superior.

Rogers settled back in his chair, leaned his elbows on its arms and steepled his fingers in front of his face as he scrutinized her. With a heavy sigh, he popped forward in his chair again and said, "I'll work things around, Roni. Would three days be enough time?"

Three days and so much to do. But any more time away was likely to attract too much attention. As it was, her leaving now would cause tongues to wag.

"I hope so, sir," she said. Without waiting for any additional confirmation, she walked to the door, but before she reached it, her captain said, "You and Trey stay safe."

She looked at him over her shoulder and nodded. "We will."

She hurried from his office and over to her cubicle. Her new partner, Heath Williams, was sitting at a small desk a few feet away from hers and talking on the phone. As she walked past him, he nodded his head in greeting, but his look grew puzzled as she packed up her knapsack.

He quickly ended the call and walked over. "What's up, Lopez?"

She finished stuffing her notes into the bag and zipped it up. "I'm sorry to spring this on you so last minute, but I'm taking a few days off."

Williams shook his head in disbelief and dragged a hand through his longish sandy hair in frustration. "Now? In the middle of all this?"

"Like I said, I'm sorry. It's personal," she said and slung her knapsack over her shoulder.

"And what am I supposed to do in the meantime? You're the lead detective on this case," he said, his voice overly loud, causing some heads to pop up as he followed her out of the squad room.

She turned and stopped him with a frigid look. "We agreed that you were going to reinterview our first witness to see if she's thought of anything else."

Williams jammed his hands on his hips. "And then what?"

Roni pulled her cell phone from her pocket and wagged it to remind him she was always in reach. "Write up an interview report and send it to me. Get the names of the hotel and club staff members working when the college students and the other women were taken. Call me to set up the next steps."

His lips tightened at her instructions. In the short time they'd worked together, she'd discovered that he didn't much like having to answer to someone else, especially a woman. But that was the price to be paid for moving up and out of the Vice Division.

She lifted a brow at his prolonged silence and did something she hardly ever did. She pulled rank. "Is there something else, Sergeant Williams?"

An angry muscle ticked along his jaw and his face mottled with blotches of angry white and red. "Nothing else, Detective Lopez. Enjoy your vacation," he bit out, making the last word sound like a curse.

She ignored him and rushed out of the squad room, but not before seeing a few thumbs up from some of the women at their desks.

The heat and humidity of a Miami afternoon hit her as soon as she left the air-conditioned building, but it was nothing compared to the blast of desire at the sight of Trey casually sitting on one of the bollards in front of the station. Waiting for her, but not in the way she'd wanted for oh so long.

She strode to him and wished that his eyes, those marvelous eyes that were the color of the Caribbean, weren't hidden behind his sunglasses.

"Everything go okay?" he asked and slowly straightened to his six feet plus height. She didn't miss the wince as he did so, confirming to her that he was still in pain from his wounds.

"Fine. We have three days," she said and kept on walking, heading for his vintage red Camaro SS.

"Three days?" he said, a little taken aback, but then he shrugged and followed her to the car.

She paused and stared at him. "That's it? Doesn't anything faze you?"

He popped the locks, but before getting in, tipped his sunglasses down with one finger and stared at her intently with that too cool blue gaze.

"I can think of one thing that does."

Idiot. Why'd you say that to her? he chastised himself and hurried into the car.

She was silent as she slipped into the passenger seat beside him, but there was no denying the tension in the vehicle. Determined to work past it, he said, "Sophie and Rob are expecting us. We're meeting them at South Beach Security."

She shot him a side-eyed glance. "You're okay with working with SBS?"

He shrugged. "As okay as I'll ever be. Besides, as much as I don't want to admit it, we're going to need their help with this case."

"Because we don't know who to trust," she said, and again he noted something in her tone that was worrisome.

"We don't. Besides each other, right?" he said, pushing on the issue to gauge her response.

"Each other and your family. But we only have three days, Trey. Is that enough?" she said, worry alive in her voice.

He shot her a quick glance and couldn't fail to miss how she was worrying her lower lip. Her hands were clenched in her lap, fingers white with pressure. Reach-

ing over, he covered her hands with his and gave a reassuring squeeze.

"We'll make it be enough," he said as he drove toward the causeway and downtown Miami. When one
of the art deco buildings in the landmarked downtown
area had been severely damaged during a hurricane and
had to be torn down, the Gonzalez family had bought
the property. They had then built a larger and more
modern building on the lot, but in the art deco style to
keep the historical look of the area.

Using his pass, Trey pulled into the private parking garage beneath the South Beach Security building
and parked in a space that was reserved for him by a
family who hoped he'd one day join them in the family business.

He turned to her and said, "Are you ready?"

IN RONI'S MIND the bigger question was if *he* was ready
to get his family's help.

His family had made their intentions known for years
that they wanted Trey out of the police force and working with them. They had made that desire even more
clear in the week since Trey had nearly been killed.

In truth, this wasn't the only time they'd been worried about Trey over the years. First, as he did his Marine deployments in Iraq and after, when he'd joined
the force and begun working undercover in some of
the department's riskier operations once he'd moved
up in the precinct.

Much like his family, Roni wished he'd find something less risky to do, which was funny really since she
was the one whose life was now in jeopardy.

"Roni? You okay?" he pressed.

She nodded. "I'm okay and I appreciate that you're willing to ask your family to help me."

"Help us, Roni. We both have something on the line here," he said and cupped her cheek. "We both want you to be safe and we both want to get to the truth."

She wanted to ask him if that was all but warned herself that things were dangerous enough with letting it get too personal.

"The truth? What if we find out Doug was dirty? What then?"

Trey's full lips thinned to a knife-sharp edge. "Then we deal with it. It's all we can do."

He rushed from the car with a slight hitch in his step, but still fast enough to force her to quicken her pace as they hurried up the stairs to the main lobby of the building. The security guard at the reception desk caught sight of them, waved and opened the gate to grant them access to the elevator bank.

The main offices for South Beach Security were on one of the topmost floors of the building while the lower levels housed a number of their different departments as well as some independent tenants.

No matter how often she visited, she was taken aback by the lushly appointed offices with the floor-to-ceiling windows that offered amazing views of downtown Miami and beyond that, Biscayne Bay and the Miami beaches.

A young Latina woman sat behind a large, ebony-colored Spanish colonial table that had been turned into a receptionist's desk. At the sight of the two of them, she smiled, rose and gestured in the direction of one of the rooms. "Everyone is waiting for you, Detective Gonzalez. Detective Lopez," she said with a warm smile.

"Everyone, Julia?" Trey said with a lift of a dark brow.

With a little wince and obviously chagrined, Julia said, "Almost everyone. Your *abuelos* aren't here...yet."

His grandparents weren't there yet, but that meant everyone else was? Roni thought, not sure she was ready for the gauntlet of facing the entire Gonzalez family at one time.

From the immediate tension in Trey's body, it was obvious he wasn't ready for it either, but there was little choice. To go it alone without his family's resources would be way too difficult and too dangerous since they didn't know who they could trust in the police department. Plus, they were racing against the clock to save the two missing college students.

He walked over to the door and opened it for her. Sure enough, a good chunk of the Gonzalez family members who made up SBS were there, along with other family members who sometimes assisted in their assorted cases.

Carolina and Mia sat at the conference room table along with his younger brother Ricky and their Whitaker cousins, Josefina—Sophie to family—and Robert, the computer gurus. There was no mistaking the Gonzalez genes in all of them, from their dark hair and light eyes to the Roman noses and thumb-print dimples in their chins.

Trey's father, Ramon, Jr, known as *Ramoncito* to the family, was at the head of the table. Trey was the third Ramon, hence his nickname.

Even at 62, Trey's father was a physically imposing

man with broad shoulders and a waist with little hint of flab. His dark hair was beginning to show a faint touch of silver at his temples, giving him a dignified look befitting the head of one of Miami's more prominent families.

Trey's mother Samantha sat kitty-corner to her husband. She had been a stay-at-home mom for Trey and his siblings. Since the kids had grown and fled the nest, Samantha had become a mother hen to those in the agency and often helped in various roles in the office. She was a pretty woman, with long brown hair drawn up in a simple topknot and striking green eyes.

"Now I have an idea how the Spanish Inquisition might have started," Trey teased, but anger and concern tangled through his voice.

"I'm sorry, Trey. Once *Tio Ramoncito* heard that you needed our help, we couldn't contain it," Sophie said.

"I'll take the blame, Josefina. Please join us, Trey. Veronica," his father said and held out a hand in invitation.

Trey walked over and hugged his mother, Sophie, Carolina and Mia. Shook hands with his father, cousin Rob, and his brother Ricky.

She hoped that was a sign that no matter how angry or worried he might be about his family's meddling, things would stay civil. Mia had mentioned more than once that Trey and his father had sometimes not talked for days after fights about Trey and his future with the family business.

Slightly relieved, she worked her way around the table, greeting everyone, grateful for whatever support they could provide during their investigations.

When she neared Trey, he offered her a tight smile and gestured to an empty chair at the large conference room table. Once she was seated, he took the spot beside her and said, "I appreciate you all being here. But I would have rather reached out to you individually when and if we needed your assistance."

"Honey, you know we only want what's best for you," his mother said, her tone placating. Her hand outstretched in pleading.

With a heavy sigh, Trey nodded. "I know that and again, I appreciate your support, *mami*. To be honest, things have changed drastically since I first called Sophie and Rob." He risked a quick glance at Roni, as if seeking her permission, and at her nod, he continued.

"We think someone tried to run down Roni today, probably because she saw something she shouldn't have the night that Doug was killed. We need more than just Sophie and Rob's help. That is, if you're willing to give it."

With a blustery toss of his hands, *Ramoncito* said, "*Mi'jo*, of course we're willing to help in any way we can. I'm just glad your stubbornness didn't keep you from asking."

She was close enough to Trey to feel the eruption of tension in his body with his father's words. But Trey's response was precisely calm and slightly chilly. "*Gracias, papi.* I guess we should get down to business, then."

Chapter Five

Trey followed his mother as she led them to an apartment on the penthouse level above the floor for the main offices for South Beach Security. The apartment was normally used for important visitors or when one of the Gonzalez family members had to stay for an exceptionally late night. It had a private elevator to the main floor next to the private offices for the Gonzalez family members and a large technology center where Sophie and Rob worked. There were two other floors below the main one where assorted SBS employees worked.

"We thought this might be the best place for you to stay while you're doing your investigations," Samantha said and gestured to the luxuriously appointed apartment.

"This isn't necessary, *mami*," Trey said, both embarrassed and worried. His mother tended to put the mother in *smother*. Add to that the close proximity to a Roni who was all grown-up and too sexy for her own good...

"You and Roni will be safe here, honey. The Twins are going to pick up some things for both of you at the store, so no need to worry about getting anything. And if you do need more food, clothing or whatever, we'll send one of the interns for it," she said and handed him the key card to the secure apartment.

"Thank you, Mrs. Gonzalez. And thank everyone else also. This is more than either Trey or I could have expected," Roni said graciously, although he suspected she was feeling as steamrollered by this as he was.

"You're welcome. Like we discussed, Sophie and Rob will be up shortly to work with you. Ricky may pop by as well in case you need to chat," his mother said and with a quick peck on his cheek and Roni's, she rushed off to the elevator.

Once she was gone, Roni looked at him in puzzlement. "Ricky? Psychologist Ricky? Is he going to help us with a profile?"

Trey shook his head. "Not in his wheelhouse normally. I think they're all worried that I may not be handling Doug's death well, but the department set up counseling for me," he admitted with a quick dip of his head.

She pinned him with her hazel-eyed gaze. "Are you handling it? While we're talking about it, how are you handling almost getting killed?"

Offhandedly he said, "Wouldn't be the first time I've been shot or almost killed. Marine, remember?"

She surprised him then, shoving her hand against his chest. Golden fire in her gaze. "Don't be so glib, Trey. Your family worries about you. They want to see you safe and happy."

He snared her hand and with a strong tug that had her off-balance, drew her near. Her softer body melted flawlessly against his, rousing instant desire. "And what about you, Roni? Do you worry? Do you want me to be safe and happy?"

The ding of the elevator warned that Sophie and Rob had arrived.

Coughing, he released her, and they jerked apart, but not before Trey whispered, "We're not done with this."

WE ARE SO DONE, she wanted to say, but bit it back. There was no way she was going to allow her attraction to him to distract them from everything else they had to focus on.

Sophie and Rob walked off the elevator, laptops tucked under their arms. They headed straight to a large dining table in the open space area of the penthouse apartment and Roni slung her knapsack over her shoulder and headed there as well.

As Trey's cousins powered up their laptops, she pulled out her notes, and Trey sauntered over to join them. Sophie and Rob sat together on one side of the table while Trey sat at the head. She could picture him in a similar position as the leader of SBS one day, the way his family wished.

She took a spot to his right and laid her notes out across the surface of the table.

"You mentioned you needed us to get information about some bank accounts," Sophie said, and at that, Roni passed her the copies IAD had given Trey with the details on the bank deposits.

"IAD thinks those monies were illegal payments to my partner Doug Adams," Trey advised and gestured to the papers.

"And you don't believe that?" Rob asked, his tones gentle and non-condemning.

"We don't," Roni said. "But there was something wrong with Doug the night he was killed. I saw him with this man," she added and handed over the police sketch of the suspect.

"I guess you think that what Trey and his partner discovered that night is related to your investigation into the missing college students?" Sophie asked while she perused the police sketch and then handed it to Rob.

Trey nodded. "We do. We also think this man tried to run down Roni because she saw him that night. If we can find out who he is, who employs him—"

"You may find out who's behind the human trafficking ring and the missing women," Sophie finished for him.

"And the attack on Roni," Trey added and glanced at her. Although he hadn't said the words, she understood. Finding him might also avoid any additional attempts to kill her, but even though they were sitting in the protective embrace of his family, she didn't intend to stay in hiding. She intended to do whatever it took to find out who was behind these crimes.

"Don't worry about me. We need to focus on finding out who is behind all this," she said and laid out the pictures of the missing college students. She pointed to each one and said, "These women are what's important. Them and Doug's family. We can't let his wife and children think that he was a criminal."

Sophie and Rob nodded in unison, so much alike that she had often thought that they were twins despite their nearly two-year age gap. And despite being the younger sibling, Sophie always struck Roni as the one in charge.

The two cousins exchanged a look before Sophie said, "We get it. We'll start with the bank account but understand that we may find that these were real deposits from a criminal enterprise."

In a soft but commanding tone, Trey said, "You won't. I knew Doug. I trusted Doug. He wasn't dirty."

A shared look passed between Sophie and Rob again. "We will do our best to get to the bottom of this."

"What about the police sketch? Do you think there's something you can do with that?" Roni asked, gesturing to the drawing that Rob was perusing.

"Is this as accurate as you can make it?" he asked and held the sketch up for them to give a last look.

With a shrug, Roni said, "It is. I'm fairly sure this is the man I saw the night Doug was killed and who was driving the car that tried to hit me earlier today."

Rob nodded and laid down the drawing. "We'll get it scanned and clean it up. After, we can use facial recognition software to try and get a hit."

"But you don't have access to our police databases. Or do you?" Trey said with a surprised lift of a brow.

Sophie bit her lip and with a strangled laugh said, "We're ethical hackers remember, Trey. There are so many public photos available on the Internet and social media that we may not need to go any further than that to find your suspect."

"You can run your software against all those public social media photos?" Roni asked, surprised by that fact.

"We can and we will. It's amazing how people complain about a lack of privacy and yet share so much about themselves online," Rob said with a rueful shake of his head.

The elevator dinged, warning them of more visitors. A second later Carolina and Mia emerged, chatting playfully, carrying way too many shopping bags. They strolled to a nearby sofa and dropped the bags on it before joining them at the dining room table.

"It looks like you cleared out a few stores," Trey teased as he took note of the pile on the sofa. Several of the bags were from some of Miami's trendiest designer shops.

Mia rolled her eyes. "If you're going to be stuck here for a few days—"

"We're not going to be stuck here. We're going to continue with our investigations no matter where they take us," Roni said and waited for Trey's disapproval as Carolina and Mia looked at him, as if waiting for him to deny her statement.

He threw his hands up in the air and said, "Roni's right. We won't take unnecessary chances, but we can't hole up here if we're going to find out what's going on."

She released a sigh of relief but tried to soothe her friends' concerns. "We appreciate all that you've done and will do. And we won't risk ourselves or any of you in the process."

"What's the plan?" Carolina said and folded her arms across her chest and a brightly colored linen blouse, designer if Roni had to guess. Carolina and Mia often received clothing and other items in exchange for mentions on their popular lifestyle blog and social media channels. With a glance at the bags on the sofa, she wondered if that was how they had amassed so many items in so short a time.

As for the plan, if it was up to Roni, they'd head back out to the club where she'd spotted the suspect with Doug. With a quick look at Trey, who seemed to understand what was unsaid, she said, "We hit the streets like we normally would. We try to find the suspect and Trey's informant."

"How can we help?" Mia said, but Trey shook his head vehemently.

"You help by staying out of that club right now," he said, and his tone warned he didn't want to be challenged.

Hesitantly, Carolina said, "Agreed. But we will keep an eye out for him."

"If you do see him, you will call us immediately and not do anything stupid," Trey said, pointing a finger between the two women in warning.

Mia snagged his finger and shook it playfully, obviously to lighten the mood. "We heard and will obey, *hermano*."

Trey, Sophie, and Rob all blew out disbelieving laughs at her comment, causing Carolina and Mia to roll their eyes, almost in unison, confirming their nicknames by appearing so much like twins with their actions.

"We should go and get to work. The computers downstairs are much more powerful," Sophie said, as she closed her laptop and stood. Robbie followed suit and after sharing goodbyes, they headed to the elevator for the trip to their tech center on the main floor.

"If you plan on going out tonight, maybe we should

grab a bite?" Mia said and whipped out her cell phone. "I can order up some things from one of the local places?" she asked but didn't wait for a reply.

Roni had dined with the Twins often enough over the years for them to know her likes and presumably Trey's. But then again, a simple order of *Cubanos*, assorted plantains and shakes wouldn't be turned down by anyone.

When she had finished placing the order, Trey shook his head. "You are something, Mia." His tone was filled with brotherly indulgence.

"*Vamos, Ramoncititico.* Carolina and I just want to be helpful," she said, teasing him with a very diminutive version of his name.

"You can be helpful by staying out of the way. Both of you," he said and warned them again with jab of a finger.

It dragged a laugh from Roni and an irate look from Trey. "I'm serious, Roni."

"I know you are, Trey. But Carolina and Mia are grown women you can't boss around. Even if you are only doing it to protect them," she chastised and shot a warning look at her two friends.

"We hear and obey," Carolina said with a teasing bow and wave of her hands.

To head off any more issues between the siblings and cousin, Roni shot to her feet and said, "Time to set the table."

Carolina and Mia immediately followed her to the kitchen area where the three of them scrounged around to find placemats, plates, glasses and cutlery while Trey rounded up sodas to serve in addition to the shakes that Mia had ordered.

Barely a few minutes later, Mia's phone chirped to say she had a text message. After a quick look, she said, "Food is down in the lobby. I'll go get it."

Trey held up a hand. "No need. I'll take care of it."

He rushed to the elevator, leaving the three women alone.

Caroline and Mia immediately launched a volley of questions at her.

"Is it really as bad as he says?" Mia asked as she walked to the dining room table with a handful of plates.

"Do you think you can handle being with him here?" Carolina tossed out, hands full of cutlery and napkins.

"Yes, and yes. More importantly, you both need to stay away from that club," she reiterated, worried that they might become targets if the suspect made the connection between them and Trey. Trey had tried hard to hide his identity when he'd gone undercover, but that secrecy might have been compromised due to recent news reports about Doug's death and Trey's shooting.

They each held up a hand as if swearing on a Bible or taking a Girl Scout pledge. "We promise. The last thing we want is to distract you by having you worry about us," Carolina said.

"That's much appreciated," Roni said as she laid out placemats on the table and the ding of the elevator warned of Trey's return.

Mia leaned close and whispered, "Promise me one thing, Roni."

"What?" Roni whispered back.

"Don't waste this opportunity with Trey."

Chapter Six

What were they thinking? Roni asked herself as she smoothed the skintight red fabric across her waist and hips.

But given Mia's last words to her before dinner, she should have expected as much from her best friends.

Not that she hadn't worn revealing clothes before while on an assignment—she just hadn't had Trey working beside her.

Walking to the door of the bedroom, she cringed when she caught a glimpse of herself in the mirror and noted how her breasts almost spilled out of the top.

You can do this, she told herself and hurried into the open space area where Trey sat on the sofa, waiting for her. His eyes widened and his gaze grew heated when he saw her, igniting warmth at her center. He schooled his reaction and she spread a hand across her midsection to calm the butterflies in her core at the sight of him. He wore an off-white linen *guayabera* that stretched across his broad shoulders and tapered inward to his lean waist and hips.

"Have you heard from Sophie and Rob?" she asked, wanting to keep things professional between them.

Trey nodded. "They're still hard at work. They hope to have something for us by tomorrow."

"Great. Where do you want to go first?" she asked, worried that since their suspect had gotten a good look at her earlier that day, it would be hard to blend in at the club where she had seen him with Doug.

"I took another look at your notes, and the two women we rescued advised that someone took them from some nicer hotels to a private party," he said, emphasizing the party part with air quotes.

Roni nodded and smoothed her hands across her hips again. "Heath and I had only just identified the two hotels the women had visited the night they were drugged. I have him working on getting lists of any staff that might have been on duty around the time that the women were taken so we can interview them."

"I guess we can start at the first hotel and get a feel for the crowd there as well as the staff. Maybe nose around until Williams can provide the information only... Can we trust anything that he gives us?" Trey asked.

TREY PEERED AT her as emotions flitted across her face. Uncertainty. Determination. Sadness. "I wish I could, only... Heath was the only one I told I was going to Barnacle Bill's."

Trey considered that and with a dip of his head, he said, "I guess we should add getting his cell phone records to what Sophie and Rob are doing."

Roni shook her head, lips pursed in disgust. "He's only been my partner for a couple of weeks, but enough for me to know he's smart. If he made a call, I'd put money on him using a burner phone."

"True," Trey said and nodded. "Let's head to the hotel and nose around. See what's happening. If there are these kinds of private parties going on, someone has to know more about them."

"And if they do?" Roni asked and smoothed her hands across her hips again in a seeming attempt to draw the fabric down just a little more. The action totally failed and only served to draw attention to the long, muscled length of her legs in the oh-so-high heels.

His gut tightened in reaction, and he sucked in a slow breath to rein in his desire and answer her question. "If the intent of the parties is to draw in attractive women, well…" He coughed into his hand and looked away. "You'd fit the bill pretty nicely."

"I—I guess we should go, then," she said, and as she walked past him, he couldn't fail to see the telltale color on her cheeks, but then again, his own were hot with embarrassment.

It made him wonder if involving her in his investigation had been a horrible idea. But she was smart, and their cases were clearly overlapping. And after the attempt on her life, there was no way he was going to leave her to fend for herself.

Not that she would want his protection. If anything, she'd hate the fact because she'd think herself capable of protecting herself. And maybe she was, but he wasn't about to take that chance.

He followed her headlong rush into the elevator, down to the main office floor where one of their nighttime security guards stood sentry by the reception desk. The man nodded as they walked over to the public elevator bank and rode it down to the parking garage.

The Camaro SS sat where they'd left it earlier that day, but he hesitated.

Roni turned to look at him when he stopped. "Something wrong?"

"If someone's been watching, they may know what I'm driving. We can take one of the company cars instead. Wait here," he said and walked toward a nearby booth. After Trey had a quick word with the guard manning the booth, the man handed him a key and gestured in the direction of a low-slung, charcoal gray BMW convertible parked by the far wall of the garage.

"Gracias," he said to the man, walked to the car, got in and wheeled it around to pick up Roni where she waited for him.

Her perfectly manicured eyebrows shot up at the sight of the car and then she fired a nervous look at her dress again. With a shrug, she opened the door, stepped in and then dropped into the passenger seat, tugging at the hem of her dress to hide her legs.

The heat of desire snaked through his gut again at the sight of all that creamy skin, but he battled it back. *This is Veronica*, he told himself. *Annoying little Veronica who tagged after you and Ricky as a kid. Carolina and Mia's best friend.*

And an amazing and beautiful woman, the little voice challenged.

Forcing away those thoughts, he said, "I still haven't been able to reach Eddie. We may need to have someone track his phone."

"Do you think he's still alive?" Roni asked and worried her lower lip.

Trey shook his head and shrugged. "I don't know.

But if he is, he may know more about whoever is behind this human trafficking."

"And where my missing college students may be," Roni added with a frustrated shake of her head.

"Yes, especially where they might be," Trey confirmed with a nod as he pulled onto the causeway to take them back toward South Beach.

There was volume on the road as they drove past Terminal Island and memories assailed him of the night of the shooting. Hands tight on the wheel, he continued past the exclusive Venetian Islands, home to some of the most expensive homes in Miami and the Gonzalez family enclave.

As he came off the causeway and drove toward Ocean Drive, traffic slowed considerably, which was typical for a Friday night in South Beach. He detoured to Collins and rode it down to one of the larger hotels, the Del Sol, where he pulled in front of a valet station. He handed off the key and hurried around to open the door for Roni and help her from the car.

Arm in arm, they walked toward the entrance and up the carpeted stairs into the hotel. There was a small lobby in the building, which was an eclectic mix of modern and eighteenth-century French flourishes. They continued into the bar area, which opened to a pool deck where a dance party was already underway.

He shot a quick look at Roni, who tipped her head in the direction of the pool deck. Playing the part of the loving couple, they joined the dancers there, moving to the beats. A DJ at the far end of the pool mixed the music pouring loudly from speakers positioned all around the area.

But even as they danced, he scanned the crowd, searching for their suspect or any signs that something was amiss. A peek at Roni confirmed that she was doing the same thing. Her hazel-eyed gaze skipped all around the location, searching. Vigilant.

He returned to his own surveillance, noting the way one of the waiters in the bar kept on delivering drinks to tables of single women, seemingly at the behest of a man at the bar. Behavior that might be normal in a situation where a man might want to meet an attractive woman, except this was going on way too often and with too many women.

The man was dressed in an expensive silk suit and an electric white shirt open to midchest. Trey detected a hint of a gold chain, and as the man waved at a bartender, he exposed an expensive gold watch on one wrist. Dark blond hair was cut short on the sides, but longer up top in strands plastered in place with gel. He looked like many of the other men at the bar, but something told Trey that there was something off. Plus, the man had the same general look as the suspect in their sketches.

When Roni laid a hand on his arm, drawing his attention, she inclined her head in the direction of the bar and the man he had noticed.

"He looks a lot like our suspect," she said in a soft whisper.

"Is he the man you saw that night? The one in the car?" Trey asked.

She clenched her jaw and did an uncertain lift of her shoulders. "I don't know. Maybe. I need to get closer."

Normally he would split away from his partner in

a situation like this, but with what had happened earlier that day, he was uneasy about doing so. He had to remind himself that she was a cop and could take care of herself. With a nod of his head, he hesitantly agreed and said, "I'll take the bartender."

"I'll try to draw out the man. See if I can get a better look."

"Give me a push," he said, and she did, playing up that they were having an argument. She shoved hard against his chest and pivoted on one high heel to walk away from him, her hips swinging in rhythm to the music. Catching the eyes of various men in and around the pool area. It ignited heat in his core and unwanted jealousy at the attention she was garnering.

Including the attention of the man at the bar.

Trey turned away from the sight of her, playing the role of the jilted boyfriend, and marched from the pool deck. But from the corner of his eye, he kept sight of Roni as she found an empty spot at a small table at the edge of the bar area.

Taking the long way around to the bar, hopefully far enough away to avoid being noticed by their possible suspect, he inched close and leaned on the marble bar. It took a few minutes for the bartender to get to him since the place was so busy.

"Seltzer with a twist of lime and mint," he said. He needed to stay sharp, especially since the aches in his shoulder and ribs where he'd been shot were coming alive. He normally held off as much as he could from taking a painkiller, but he suspected he wasn't going to be able to avoid it tonight. The pain was just building too quickly. But not until both Roni and he were safe and sound back at the South Beach Security apartment.

Fighting back the hurt, he watched as their possible suspect stared at Roni. The ghost of a smile passed across the man's face and Trey understood. A woman alone would be far easier to take than a woman who came with friends to watch over her.

Long minutes passed until the bartender, a young Latino whose name tag said Mateo, placed Trey's drink in front of him. He tossed down two twenties, earning a calculating look from the bartender.

Trey jerked his chin in the direction of their target. *"¿Quien es?"* he said, hoping the bartender knew something about him.

"What's he to you?" Mateo said, clearly defensive.

"He's eyeballing my woman, that's what," he said, forcing a harsh tone into his voice and glaring toward the man.

Mateo inched on tiptoes to peer over the edge of the bar as if to confirm what Trey was complaining about. With a shrug, he said, "He's a regular. I think he's in the penthouse suite."

Trey was about to press him for more when patrons at the far end of the bar signaled to Mateo. Without another word, he rushed off to help them and Trey returned his attention to Roni as a waiter brought her a drink that the suit had ordered.

She waved him off, refusing the drink, and Trey chuckled and sipped his seltzer.

Smart girl, he thought. Playing hard to get was bound to make the man even more interested in her. *Enough*

to get him to walk over so she could get a better look?
he wondered.

As long minutes passed, the man seemed to have accepted the rebuff without a care, especially as another
group of women accepted the round of drinks he sent
and raised them in a toast in his direction. Taking that
as an invitation, he rose and approached the table that
was only a few feet from where Roni sat.

FROM THE CORNER of her eye, Roni watched as their possible suspect mingled with a group of young women
who were clearly out for a night of fun. The women
appeared to be in their early twenties, right around the
age of the missing college students and the sex workers they had saved from their Terminal Island captivity.

Focusing on their conversation, she tried to hear what
was being said, but the music was too loud for her to
catch anything but a word here and there. In light of
that, she shifted slightly in her chair, wanting to see the
group and memorize the women's faces, just in case.

The women were typical of the crowd you'd get in
a hot spot known for its nightlife. Dressed to entice,
perfectly coiffed and made-up, and wearing the kinds
of heels that sent an obvious message. A message that
the man had clearly heard—hence the drinks and his
approach.

Turning her attention to the man, she eyed him up
and down without artifice and he noticed. He eyed her
and smiled as if to say, "Look what you're missing."

What she was missing was a very expensive bespoke
silk suit over a well-toned gym rat body. Dark eyes, almost black in the dim light, remained on her face even

as he was chatting with the young women at the table. As he realized he had Roni's full attention, he smiled, his full lips parting to reveal perfect teeth.

Those dark eyes were off. She could have sworn the man she had seen, the man with the cold dead eyes, had blue eyes. But his hair was close in color to what she remembered of their suspect. The style, however, was like that of many of the men in the club.

Is he the right man? she pressed herself, hating that she was experiencing doubt.

In that moment, she realized she had to make a split-second decision. Engage him or turn away. *Make the call, Roni*, she told herself.

Chapter Seven

Roni shoved herself to her feet, grabbed her clutch and hurried away from their target and the women busily fawning over him.

She swore she could feel the man eyeing her as she hurried toward the bar, making sure that Trey noticed what she was doing. Hopefully he would shortly follow at a discreet distance.

Pushing through the patrons headed in the direction of the bar and the pool dance party beyond that, she quickly moved toward one side of the lobby where she'd likely be out of sight.

She guessed she had done a good enough job when Trey reached the lobby and stopped abruptly, clearly having lost sight of her. But with a sharp look around, he found her and marched to her side.

"Did you get a good look at him?" Trey asked, but as he did so, Roni caught sight of the man and the women heading toward the elevators. Grabbing hold of Trey's waist, she inched him in front of her and whipped out her phone, using his big body to screen her. She snapped off a burst of photos, hoping that some of them would be clear enough to identify the man.

"I did, but I'm still not sure," she said, suddenly doubting her own memory of the man she had seen with Doug and the one who had tried to run her down. It had all happened too fast. Much too fast.

Shaking her head, she said, "Maybe we'll have some clear photos to show our victims. Maybe they can either confirm or deny that this is our suspect."

Trey peered over his shoulder at the entourage as they stepped into the elevator. As soon as the doors had closed, Trey said, "The bartender I talked to thinks the man is in the penthouse suite."

"We can ask the desk for his name, but legally they can tell us to go pound sand," she said as Trey shifted to allow her a glimpse of the people coming and going in the lobby.

"They could, but maybe there's another way," he said and walked to the housephone, Roni chasing after him.

He picked up the phone, dialed the operator and said, "*Hola*, I was hoping you could help me. I have a delivery for Mr. Henderson in the penthouse suite. At least I think that's his name. It's really smudged on the address slip."

She couldn't make out what was being said at the other end, but then Trey said, "Are you sure? It's Mr. Wilson in the penthouse suite? Do you have a Mr. Henderson staying with you at all?"

Another quick burst of noise came across the line, apparently with enough information for Trey to end the call. "I appreciate it. I'll have to check with the sender. *Gracias*."

"Wilson? Any first name?" Roni wondered as she walked beside Trey across the lobby, his big hand splayed at the small of her back again. The touch possessive and protective all at once.

"John," Trey replied.

Roni shook her head. "There could be thousands of people with that name."

With a quick dip of his head, Trey said, "And that's assuming it's not an alias. But hopefully you got a good photo that we'll be able to run through the facial recognition software."

"Hopefully," she said as they stepped outside and down the stairs to the valet area. The delay while they were waiting for their car had her peering up at the tower of the hotel and second-guessing herself. "Do you think I was wrong to blow him off?"

TREY TILTED HIS head to one side and jammed his hands into his pants pockets, considering her carefully before he answered. Then with a strong nod, he said, "I trust your judgment, Roni. Especially with all that's happened. Once we know more about Mr. Wilson, we can decide how to proceed."

The tension and indecision fled her body with his words. "*Gracias.* Do you want to check out the second hotel Williams and I identified?"

"It makes sense. This activity with Wilson could be just a coincidence. I doubt it, but it's possible," he said, urging Roni in the direction of the car as the valet drove to the curb. He held the door open and provided her a steadying hand. She slipped into the seat, displaying an enticing length of leg once again.

He forcefully looked away, swung around and into the driver's seat. Pulling away from the curb, he drove to the lower-numbered streets off Ocean Drive and Collins. Because of the difficulty of parking on Ocean Drive, they'd have to walk to the second hotel that Roni and her partner had identified.

Unfortunately, that meant circling until he found a parking spot a few blocks from the hotel. It worried him to have Roni exposed for that long, but hopefully whoever had tried to run her down had not had a chance to follow them from the South Beach Security location. Regardless, he kept his head on a swivel and Roni tucked close to his side where he could shield her.

Luckily, he didn't pick up on anything as they made the short walk and entered the hotel, which was a few doors down from the location they had been surveilling on the night Doug had been killed. It made him wonder if their unsub chose his possible victims not at this hotel, but at the club where Roni had seen him with Doug.

"Something wrong?" Roni asked, looking at him.

He hadn't realized that he'd tensed up with those thoughts. "I'm fine, only… Are you sure this is one of the places where your unsub selected his women?"

There was no mistaking how Roni stiffened with the question, clearly seeing it as a challenge. "I'm as positive as I can be based on the victims' interviews. Do you doubt me?"

"I don't. I trust you," he said, but she pressed him on it.

"Do you? Do you think I made the right call before? Letting a possible suspect go?" she challenged.

If they were going to accomplish anything over the three days that they had for their investigation, there couldn't be any doubts between them. "I think you made the right call. We need more info on Wilson before we go off half-cocked."

"I agree," she said, but curtly, still stung by his earlier question.

Because of that, as they neared the hotel, he leaned close and said, "You lead. I'll follow."

She jumped against him, but then the tightness in her body fled as quickly as air from a popped balloon. With a hurried peek, almost as if to confirm that she'd heard him correctly, she said, "First stop, the bar."

He followed her, protecting her back as they swam through the ocean of bodies on the dance floor and mingling by the bar. Once she sat on a stool, he slipped in behind her, once again shielding her with his body.

His proximity was both distracting and comforting. She focused on the latter and scanned the nightclub for any sign of their suspect or any other kind of unusual behavior. Unlike at the earlier hotel, nothing was making her radar ping.

There were dozens of gorgeous young women at the bar and on the dance floor, unaware of the danger they might be in. Women just out for a good time the way she and her friends often went out on a weekend.

They ordered drinks, seltzers for both, and after about half an hour, she took his hand and led him toward another area in the club. There were a number of tables there packed with an assortment of patrons that reflected the diversity of South Beach in every imaginable way. Both gay and straight men and women, in couples or not. Locals and tourists of every race, mixed or not.

She led Trey to a more intimate corner, drew him to her side and went on tiptoe to whisper in his ear, "I'm not seeing anything. You?"

He laid a big hand on her waist, angling his body to partially cover hers while turning to watch the dance floor and in and around the bar. "*Nada.* Maybe we should try La Luna?" he said, referring to the location where she'd seen Doug with their suspect.

That was probably the last place their unsub might be, given the attention he had drawn to himself, but there was clearly nothing going on here. "Sure. We may get lucky."

They walked together through the club and lobby, vigilant for any signs they might have missed. On the sidewalk, he once again assumed a position to protect her, and they hurried a few doors down to La Luna. It was as busy as the other locations, and they took their time scoping out the bar and dance floor. Moved from one area to the next, cops' eyes on the lookout for anything out of the ordinary, but with no luck.

They had exited the club and were walking into the temporary pedestrian area on Ocean Drive when Trey paused, reached into his pants pocket and pulled out his cell phone. He pressed a finger against one ear to combat the noise from the clubs as he brought the phone up to the other.

She waited, impatient, but hoping it was good news. When the barest hint of a smile flitted across his lips and he nodded, it confirmed what she had hoped.

He swiped to end the call and faced her, still smiling. "Facial recognition software got a hit from an old photo on a high school yearbook site. Sophie and Rob are doing an age progression as we speak to see if an older version matches the sketch we have. They've also got some more info on the bank accounts."

"Time to head back to SBS," she said and hustled to return to their car.

He fell into step beside her, teasing her with, "I like a woman who knows what she wants."

She shook her head, certain he was teasing, but also imagining what he might think if she did what she wanted to do with him. But as she'd warned herself before, she couldn't let him distract her.

At least, not now. But once this case was over, she intended to show him exactly what she wanted.

TREY WAS VIGILANT the entire drive to the South Beach Security building, constantly checking the rearview mirror and his surroundings for any signs that they were being followed.

Nothing.

It brought relief, but not for long, as they sat with Sophie and Rob at the dining room table in the penthouse and his cousins worked through what they had found.

"The good news is that we got a hit," Sophie said. She pulled up the yearbook photo that had been uploaded to a website and projected it onto the wall of monitors at one side of the room, using a laser pointer to point out the suspect's name and face. With the click of a button, his face morphed from the boyish look of a high school senior to someone harder and older.

"That definitely looks like our suspect," Roni said with a harsh laugh. "Amazing," she added.

His cousins never failed to astound Trey with their

skills. The man they had identified was remarkably close in appearance to the one they'd seen at the Del Sol earlier that night. *Close, but is it close enough?* he wondered.

With a quick nod, Sophie flashed more information and photos on the screen. "Miguel Walsh. Local boy apparently. Mother escaped Cuba in the 1970s. Father is of Irish descent. Went to South Dade High School in Homestead. So-so student. Did two years in the army," she said and gestured for Rob to continue.

"Military time appears to be uneventful. After he returned from Afghanistan, he took a job as a security guard with a small agency. Mall cop kind of work. That's where things start to get dicey," Rob said. Clearing the info and photos from the monitors, he put up another set of pictures and continued with his report.

"While we were waiting for you, we did some additional investigations. Two years ago, Walsh left the security agency and went to work at the offices for MCP Enterprises. MCP was originally known as Magic City Provisions. It started in the early 1950s as a supplier of Latino food products to area bodegas and independent supermarkets. With the Cuban diaspora of the 1960s, their business boomed."

"Lots can go on in an import/export business. Who knows what they're really into," Trey said, having had at least one case where a similar business was a front for drug smuggling.

Roni chimed in. "Is it possible to track down more info on MCP? Find out who runs it and what properties they own?"

"You're thinking about the Terminal Island lot where the shipping containers were located?" Trey said.

Roni nodded and added, "Or another location where they could be hiding other women."

Sophie and Rob exchanged a look. "We can try, but I suspect the property may be in the name of a shell company," Sophie said.

"Let's go back to Walsh's job at MCP," Trey said and gestured to Walsh's photo.

"We don't have much on that yet, but we'll keep on digging," Rob said.

"Thank you. With what you've given us, we may be able to ask for a search warrant," Roni said, looking over at Trey.

Trey nodded, but despite what his cousins had uncovered, he still felt they were far away from an answer to their cases. Especially Doug's murder and the IAD investigation. "Thank you for all this, but what about the bank accounts?"

Sophie coughed uneasily, which had always been one of her tells when they played cards as kids.

"Josefina?" he said, pressing her the way he'd heard her mother do more than once when they were children.

"The money came from a numbered account in Switzerland," Sophie said, obviously uncomfortable.

"But we can get the name of the account owner, right?" Trey pushed, and Sophie coughed again and shook her head.

"If you're thinking of the government getting that information years ago it was because those particular banks had branches in the U.S. The government pressured those banks to give up the secret information or face daily fines in the millions for not doing so. But recently the Swiss have been a little more cooperative with authorities if illegal activities are suspected," she explained.

Trey's gut twisted into a knot, and he clenched his fists on the surface of the table. Roni reached over and laid a hand on his, offering comfort. "That doesn't mean Doug was dirty," she said, leaning toward him, her face filled with compassion.

"It doesn't, especially since there's something off with the deposits," Rob said, tapping some keys to bring up the bank accounts. As he spoke, Sophie highlighted the information on the monitor.

"The wires we tracked were done after Doug's death, but his accounts show they were deposited before his death," Rob explained.

"Someone doctored his accounts to try and make him look dirty?" Roni said and squeezed his hand.

"Possibly," Rob confirmed.

"But why put the money there at all? He's dead, right? Why throw that kind of money away?" Roni pressed.

"To throw us off the scent of the real dirty cop," Trey said.

Chapter Eight

Roni nodded and sat back, contemplating all that had happened since the night Doug had been killed and Trey had nearly died. Attempting to recall what she'd either said or reported to anyone in order to figure out who might be that dirty cop.

"Roni?" Trey asked, shifting in his seat slightly to examine her face.

She shook her head and said, "I don't think I mentioned seeing Doug with our unsub to anyone else. But Heath was working undercover with me that night. I don't know what he saw."

"Sounds to me like this Heath person is a possible suspect," Sophie said, and Rob added, "Maybe we should check him out as well."

"Maybe. I'll let you know," Roni said, although she felt dirty about possibly asking them to investigate her partner. Just as guilty as she was feeling about hiding the fact from Trey that she was supposedly working with IAD. Not that she'd really given them any information.

This time it was Trey comforting her by turning his hand over and twining his fingers with hers. "We have to do what's necessary to get to the bottom of this. It's not just about Doug or your safety. It's about those two missing college students and who knows how many other women."

"I get it. No stone unturned no matter how painful it might be," she said with a bob of her head and hoped he would feel the same way if he found out IAD had asked her to help with the investigation.

"Speaking of stones, we're hoping you can get us an address for Walsh and some info on a John Wilson. He's currently staying—"

"In the penthouse suite at the Del Sol," Rob immediately replied.

Roni was taken aback. "You know this man?"

"Everyone in Miami's tech industry knows John Wilson. He made a fortune selling his AI startup to Google. His big thing now is building Miami's tech sector. He's brought lots of other tech companies down to the area," Sophie explained.

"Sun, sand and no income tax. Lots of places to party," Rob said with a shake of his head.

"Like the Del Sol? He's rich?" Roni asked, wanting confirmation.

"Filthy rich, but that doesn't mean squeaky clean. You may want to talk to Carolina and Mia about him. They've been to his parties in the penthouse," Sophie said.

Trey's fingers tightened on hers at the mention of the Twins. "We will. Thanks."

Worried about what Trey would say to the Twins, she whipped out her cell phone and brought up the photos of the man who had been soliciting women to head to Wilson's penthouse.

"Do you think that these photos are clear enough for you to get a hit with the facial recognition software?" she asked and showed them the photos.

Sophie and Rob both leaned forward to look at the images.

"He looks a lot like Walsh," Rob said, and Sophie seconded his observation.

"They do look alike, but there may be enough differences to get a new hit. Email the photos and we'll get on it," Sophie said.

"In the morning. Sophie has a tendency to get lost in these things, but we need to get some rest and I imagine you do, too," Rob clarified.

Roni shot a look at the time on the phone. Just past midnight and she'd been going since six that morning. "It is time for some rest. Thank you again for all that you've done."

"*Sí, gracias.* You've given us a lot of information," Trey said and rose, wincing as he did so.

If it had been anyone else, Roni would have asked if he was okay, but she knew Trey wouldn't appreciate her calling attention to any possible vulnerability in front of his cousins.

When Trey took an unsteady step forward, she shot to her feet and swooped around to hug Sophie and Robbie and guide them toward the elevator. "Get some rest. We'll touch base in the morning."

"*Buenas noches,*" Sophie and Rob said, almost in unison, making Roni chuckle. In some ways they were as twin-like as Carolina and Mia, maybe more so since they were brother and sister.

After the elevator door closed, Roni faced Trey, who

was standing by the table, rubbing his shoulder. "You okay?"

With a shrug that had him grimacing, he said, "I need to take a painkiller, but I'm not a fan of them," he freely admitted.

"I'll get you some water," she said and hurried to the kitchen area in the large open space of the suite. She filled a glass with ice water from the fridge and handed it to him as he limped over. He took the glass from her, popped a pill into his mouth and downed the water. But as he set it in the dishwasher, he said, "I'm sorry I got you involved in this."

She shook her head and guilt again twisted her gut that she wasn't being completely truthful with him. "I was already involved, remember? Those missing women are *my* case."

With a shrug, he said, "You're right, but no one was trying to kill you."

"The moment that unsub knew that I had seen him, I was in danger," she said and laid a hand on his chest to try and soothe his upset.

He covered her hand with his and stepped closer. "I will keep you safe."

"I can take care of myself and you, Trey. We will solve this," she said, certain that together they could do almost anything.

He cupped her cheek. "We will, but at what price? Doug's reputation? Our relationship?"

She narrowed her gaze at his words. "*Our* relationship?"

He stroked his thumb across her lips, rousing unwanted emotions. Now was the absolute worst time to give in to her attraction. "I know you too well, Roni. I see it in your eyes that something's bothering you. Besides me, that is," he said with a wry smile.

With a playful shove against his chest, she said, "You're way too full of yourself, Trey."

"I am, but I'm right. Something's bothering you," he pressed.

"I guess I'm doubting myself a little. Walsh looks like our suspect. So does the man at the Del Sol. What if it was someone else behind the wheel of the car?"

He considered her carefully, his gaze traveling over her features. "We'll get to the bottom of this. Get some rest. It's going to be a long day tomorrow."

It would be a long day, especially once they had an address for Walsh, talked to the Twins about Wilson, and she connected with Williams. *The three Ws*, she thought with a silent laugh, but maybe by the end of tomorrow they'd know more.

"Good night, Roni. Sweet dreams," he said and brushed a quick kiss on her cheek before he walked away.

She watched him go but knew her dreams would be anything but sweet if they included Trey.

THE SMELL OF coffee woke him from a troubled sleep filled with images of the night Doug had been killed and the car barreling toward Roni.

He flipped onto his back in bed, gritting his teeth as his shoulder and ribs protested the movement. The doctors had told him it would take time to fully heal but he hated being less than one hundred percent, especially when Roni's life was at stake.

Not to mention the Twins. He was unhappy that they were regulars at the clubs where the women were disappearing and that they might have connections to Wilson. Like Sophie had said, filthy rich didn't mean squeaky clean. There had been too many recent cases of wealthy individuals involved with the sexual abuse of women.

Especially sex workers like the ones who were rescued on that fateful night. Women who were invisible, which was probably why no one had reported them missing. It was that kind of invisibility that had allowed people like the Green River Killer and the Long Island Serial Killer to get away with their crimes for so long.

And if Eddie hadn't tipped him off, those women might have been sold into slavery.

Eddie, he thought, and swiped his cell phone off the nightstand. It had been a little over a week since he'd been able to speak to his informant. The only thing that gave him hope that he was still alive was the fact that Eddie's body hadn't turned up somewhere. But then again, he could be in the belly of an alligator down in the Everglades.

Despite those concerns, he dialed Eddie again and as it had before, the call immediately went to voice mail. In a way, that was a relief because he suspected that if Eddie wasn't clearing out his voice mails, the mailbox might be full.

He left a message asking Eddie to phone him and ended the call.

Slipping from the bed, he grabbed a T-shirt and fleece shorts from the pile of clothes Carolina and Mia had purchased for him. He'd grab a shower later, after he'd had a chance to coordinate what they were going to do today.

Exiting the bedroom, he found Roni in the kitchen, buttering some toasted Cuban bread and making *café con leches* with espresso and hot milk.

"Smells delicious," he said and covered his stomach when it growled with hunger.

She gestured in the direction of the refrigerator and cabinets. "Everything is fully stocked."

He nodded. "They always have it ready for guests and family members."

Her eyebrows shot up. "It's quite an organization that your family has here."

"It is," he said and hoped she wouldn't take the discussion to where it usually went when his family was involved, namely, that he should leave the force and join South Beach Security.

Luckily she didn't say anything more as she handed him a plate with the buttered toast and a large mug with the coffee, then set out a plate and mug for herself.

He sat on a stool at the breakfast bar, and she took a spot a few feet away on another stool. "I knew it was successful, but I guess I never realized how successful," she admitted.

He shrugged, uncomfortable with where their chat was going and hating the bite in his words as he said, "You mean the huge home on Palm Island, private schools and fancy cars wasn't a clue?"

Her lips thinned into a tight line. "Clueless, right, but to me, all I saw was this amazing loving family. And Carolina and Mia never had their noses up in the air, even after they found out I was a scholarship student. Your *abuelos* and parents either."

He couldn't deny what she said. Despite the wealth

and fame the family had achieved, they'd never acted uppity like some nouveau riche, maybe because they knew how hard it was to earn that success.

"We never let it get to our heads," he said as he dunked his toast into the coffee and then brought the sopping mess to his mouth. "Mmm, delicious. *Gracias* for prepping it."

"Had to do something while you were playing Sleeping Beauty," she teased and dunked her own bread.

"The pain pills knock me out, but you could have woken me up," he said and couldn't resist adding, "A kiss would do it, *verdad*?"

A bright stain of color flooded across her cheeks and her hand shook as she picked up her coffee cup to drink the *café con leche*.

Grinning, he raised his own cup, filled with the delicious mix of coffee, milk, sugar and the buttery remnants from the toast. As he did so, he noticed the laptop sitting on the dining room table and inclined his head in its direction. "I guess you were doing more than making breakfast."

She nodded and sipped her coffee. "I wanted to know more about this Wilson guy. Also, about the history of MCP and its owners."

"Find out anything interesting?" he asked.

A hesitant shrug came as she dipped her toast into the coffee again. "Wilson is known as a player. He owns a home in the Indian Creek section, but regularly has his parties at the Del Sol."

"I guess he doesn't want to leave trash in his own backyard," he said, thinking that it made it easier to hide evidence when you had the hotel cleaning crew coming in to cover up any mess that you'd made.

"That's very possible. Hopefully Carolina and Mia can fill us in on what happens at those parties, although there are lots of photos online. News reports. Social media posts with photos tagging him."

"I'm sure they all paint a rosy picture, but we both know that can hide real evil," he said, recalling the many photos of celebrities and politicians who had eventually been revealed as serial predators.

"We do, but my gut is telling me we should be looking toward Walsh and MCP more," she said, as she retrieved her laptop and placed it on the counter between them.

She scrolled to the company's website and said, "MCP has been family-owned for generations. The latest CEO is Aaron Santana, the grandson of the founder. Ivy League graduate. MBA. His father passed the reins to him about five years ago, but things haven't been going all that well since he took over."

"Why is that?" Trey asked.

Roni tapped a few keys and pulled up an article on a business site with the glaring headline "MCP Suffers from Loss of Mom and Pop Businesses." "They'd been supplying predominantly small grocery stores and bodegas but with the advent of big-box stores and larger grocery chains, they lost more and more of their customers. Santana began a pivot to overcome that, but the business is struggling."

"What's that old saying? The first generation sows it, the second generation grows it and the third generation

ank accounts and more info on the MCP locations.
, the ownership of the Terminal Island property."
ob followed suit and stood. "Time for us to go and
e you to your investigation," he said.

Once his cousins had left, Trey said, "Have you
ed Heath yet?"

he shook her head. "I was waiting to call him and
what he had for me on the hotel staff."

"I'm not sure we should share what we know about
lsh yet or bring him in for questioning at the mo-
nt," he said.

"I agree that we shouldn't tip our hand that we know
o he is. I'd like to see if we can get Walsh's cell phone
ords. Financials. Sunpass. All the standard things to
e where he's been and who he's been talking to," she
d, thinking of all the regular ways at her disposal as
olice officer.

"And get the phone providers to track Eddie's phone
hey can. Hopefully he's not smart enough to shut off
Wi-Fi and location services," Trey said and gestured
her phone. "I guess it's time to call Williams."

"It is and if you don't mind, I'd like to mention our
millionaire Wilson. See how he reacts and what
does with that information," she said, hoping that
'd be able to discover more about whether her new
ner was trustworthy.

like that idea since up until now, Wilson hasn't
e up during our investigations. Your partner's re-
se to that could help us."

ith that, Roni dialed her partner, who immediately
ered. "Good morning, Roni."

orning, Heath. How's it going?"

blows it," Trey said and grimaced, obviously seeing how the saying could eventually apply to his own family.

She nodded. "Not in every family, but in this case, Santana might need other ways to make up for the loss of that income. Could be money laundering. Drugs or human trafficking."

"Especially if they have a bunch of warehouses sitting around empty. Easy enough to hide all kinds of things there," he said, considering all the research that Roni had done.

"Hopefully Sophie and Rob can find out more about who owns that Terminal Island property," she said.

He gobbled down the last of his toast and jerked a thumb in the direction of his bedroom. "I'm going to take a shower and get dressed."

Roni nodded. "Hopefully your cousins can give us some more info on Walsh so we can decide what to do. I'm going to call Heath and see what he's got for us."

He arched a brow at her mention of her new partner. She immediately reacted with, "I'll be careful with what I tell him."

He nodded. "I called Eddie. His voice mail is still working, which I hope is a good thing. Maybe we can get someone at the station to triangulate Eddie's cell phone signal because we can't keep on waiting on him to get back to us."

"I'm going to try and find out more about Santana and MCP."

"I appreciate that, Roni. Working with you… You're a good cop, but then again, I think I always knew that," he said and hurried from the room, not wanting to give away more of what he was feeling about her.

Pride, but worry as well. When Carolina and Mia had told him that Roni was joining the force, that had been his first reaction. Silly, because there were a number of women on the force.

But those other women weren't Roni. *My Roni*, he had to admit, not that he'd ever done anything about his feelings for her. After Doug's death and his own shooting, it was time to reevaluate what he wanted in life. Where he was going. And although he didn't want to admit it to his family, his thoughts had gone to his possibly leaving the force for a safer profession and a more normal life.

The big question was whether that more normal life would include Roni.

Chapter Nine

Roni sat at the dining room table as Soph[ie] provided the information they'd discussed t[he day be]fore. Unfortunately, there wasn't much mor[e]

"Whoever made these bank deposits is [a sophisti]cated hacker. They've spoofed their IP addr[ess as] well," Sophie said.

"Would Wilson have been able to do t[hat?" he] asked as he glanced at the notes his cousins [laid] out for them.

Rob sat back uneasily. "Hacking is not [his] thing. He's more into AI-based algorithms [and predictive behavior modeling, but h[e's got] people working for him who could do thi[s."]

"Carolina and Mia could give you a [line on] Wilson. Maybe even get you invited to [his par]ties," Sophie said.

Roni mumbled a curse under her b[reath] ing up the invite from Wilson's goon, [it was] better to get impressions on the tech [mogul with] Trey at her side.

"We'll talk to them later," Trey sai[d as] Sophie shut down her laptop. "We'l[l

"I have the info you wanted. Hotels sent it over late last night. I'll email it to you," Heath said. In the background, she could hear the familiar sounds of activity in the squad room—the chatter of officers, phones ringing.

A swoosh from her phone alerted her to the new email in her mailbox.

"Thanks, Heath. I want to ask you for a favor. I came across an interesting guy last night at Del Sol," she offered, her gaze locking with Trey's as she spun a tale for her new partner.

"I thought you were on vacation," Heath challenged, but she sensed humor in his words and not mistrust.

"Are you ever really on vacation when you're a cop?" she teased right back and continued. "I went out for drinks with a friend, and we were invited to a party in the penthouse. Some guy named John Wilson reserves it pretty regularly, from what I gathered."

A pause came, but not overly long. "Never heard of the guy. I can ask around for you if you want."

She had to make a split-second decision, but nothing about the call so far had raised alarms about her new partner. "That would be helpful but try to keep it low-key. We don't want to spook him if there's more to it."

"Will do," he said without hesitation.

She was about to hang up when Heath said, "Did Ramirez track you down yesterday?"

She started, surprised by the question. "IAD Ramirez?" she asked, and Trey sat up higher at the mention of the cop.

"Yeah, that Ramirez. He came by asking for you right after you took a break. I told him you were at Barnacle Bill's," he said matter-of-factly, as if he'd done nothing wrong by providing the information.

"I didn't talk to him. I guess we missed each other. Thanks for the heads-up," she said and swiped to end the call.

"Ramirez wanted to talk to you?" Trey asked, narrowing his gaze to study her as she responded.

She shrugged, but the action was stilted and tense. "He and Anderson are talking to everybody about what happened that night."

Just like they had talked to him, only... His gut was telling him there was more to Ramirez's visit to see Roni and none of it was good. "Ramirez knew where you were before Walsh tried to run you down. The question is, what did he do with that information?"

Roni shook her head, clearly distressed by what he was implying, maybe because she was thinking the same thing. "You think Ramirez is the dirty cop? The one who's pointing the finger at Doug to hide his own criminality?"

Trey paced the floor as he tossed out the thoughts racing through his head. "Possibly. Now we have another suspect to add to the list. Walsh and Santana. Wilson and his slick sidekick. Your new partner. This case is getting more and more hairy every second."

"It is but we will solve it. And for the record, after chatting with Heath, I'm not sure he should be on our list," Roni said, then rose and walked over to stop his nervous pacing by laying a hand on his arm.

He met her hazel gaze. It was clear and filled with conviction. Because she was a good cop with great instincts, he trusted her assessment. "Okay, one down. Let's see what your partner can find out about Wilson.

In the meantime, I want to check out the address my cousins gave us for Walsh's residence before we head to the MCP offices."

Roni nodded. "That sounds like a good plan."

"Okay. Let's go."

WALSH'S HOME WAS in Coral Gables, one of the nicer Miami neighborhoods.

"A security guard maybe makes $40- or $50K, right?" Trey said as they parked up the block from their suspect's home. "Makes you wonder how he can afford a house like this."

Roni swiped her phone screen and pulled up data on the home. "According to this real estate website, this house is worth about $695,000. Not the kind of digs for your typical security guard."

Trey started the car and they drove past the home slowly. Roni inspected it for signs of anything unusual, but other than some well-placed security cameras, there was nothing to set it apart from the other homes on the block.

"Time to head to the MCP offices," she said and within twenty minutes they were pulling into a parking lot for the MCP building on Brickell Avenue. One of the more modern structures along the avenue, it was over twenty stories sheathed in white marble, with pale green glass windows and stainless-steel trim. All along the base of the building were lushly landscaped areas that broke up the sterility of the marble, glass and steel. Near the front door an oculus window provided a view into the gleaming marble lobby.

Roni paused there, peering inside the lobby to gauge

where the security guards might be, but the reception desk was at the farthest end of a long lobby. "Can't see anything," she said and risked a quick look at him.

He nodded. "Time to go in, but first…" He reached over and tucked a loose strand of her hair underneath the baseball cap she was wearing. Earlier that morning, they had run back by the precinct where a fellow officer had supplied fake courier jackets and caps in order for them to go undercover and hopefully keep Walsh from identifying her.

Together they entered the lobby and walked over to the reception area, all the time scanning the interior for any sign of their unsub.

Roni saw no signs of Walsh on the main level.

At the desk, the guard looked them up and down and held his hand out for the delivery, clearly intending to not let them enter the building.

"Sorry, but I've got to get a signature for this," Trey said and tapped to the spot on a fake delivery form that said, "Signature Required."

"No can do. No one goes up without an appointment," he said and shook his head. He was a large Latino man with a clean-shaven head and bulging muscles that stretched the fabric of his light blue shirt. A patch on his elbow identified the local security guard company that employed him.

Trey leaned close to the guard and jerked his head in her direction. In low pleading tones, he said, "*Mira, mano.* Don't make me look bad in front of my trainee. *Por favor.*"

The security guard looked from him to her, and then

reluctantly dipped his head and unlocked the gate for them to pass through. "Twenty-sixth floor."

They walked to the elevator bank, but the whole time Roni was scanning the lobby, memorizing as much as she could about the area. The elevator arrived quickly and after they entered, it rose speedily into another reception area where a large stainless-steel sign on one wall declared MCP Enterprises.

A receptionist sat at a large desk made of white lacquer and more stainless steel. On either side of the lobby were two security guards, but unlike the blue-shirted man in the lobby, these men were in well-tailored suits with pressed white shirts, and red-and-white striped ties.

One of them was Miguel Walsh.

It took all her willpower to not go over and cuff him. But if they wanted to find her two missing college students and who was behind the human trafficking ring, they couldn't rush. Even if she only had two more days away from the precinct before her absence was going to raise questions about what was happening with the investigation.

At the desk, Trey handed over the fake delivery envelope and the young woman said, "Turn right past the glass doors and go straight to the very end. Mr. Santana's administrative assistant will sign for it."

"Thank you," he said and gestured for her to follow him through the doors the receptionist unlocked.

They turned as the young woman had instructed and as they did so, Roni looked around, getting a feel for MCP Enterprises.

The employees walking in and around the cubicles and offices were well-dressed in business casual clothes, but there were a number of empty cubicles, making her wonder if there had been a reduction in staff due to their financial problems.

At the corner, an attractive African American woman sat at a large and imposing desk, almost as if she was standing guard, in front of a corner office where a man lounged in a chair, his back to them as he spoke on the phone. The interior and exterior walls were all glass, providing breathtaking views of the skyscrapers along Brickell and beyond them the waters of the Miami River and Biscayne Bay.

When the man turned and hung up, she was able to identify that it was Aaron Santana, the current CEO of MCP Enterprises. She had seen pictures of him as they'd done their research, but the man sprawled in the chair looked aged, troubled, given the deep furrows in his brow and along the tight lines at the edges of his lips.

He shot a quick glance in their direction, but then picked up the phone again and turned away from them.

"Busy man," she said without thinking.

In a sympathetic tone the administrative assistant said, "He's got a lot on his plate."

Probably more than his assistant could even begin to imagine.

"Thanks for your help," Trey said and laid a hand on Roni's back to urge her toward the reception area.

She followed his lead, but once again focused on her surroundings, especially as they neared the glass doors for the reception area and Walsh pushed through, his face set in stone. She shrank back, almost hiding behind Trey as Walsh hurried past.

He went straight to Santana's office, entered and closed the door behind him.

"Just your typical CEO-security guard interaction," Trey whispered in her ear and shielded her from view as they pushed through the doors to the elevator banks.

On their way down, she said, "What do you think that was all about?"

Trey shook his head. "Nothing good from the look on Santana's face."

"Walsh's car is probably in the parking lot, but we can't put a tracker on it without a warrant," Roni said.

"Maybe it's time we got one."

Chapter Ten

Trey didn't know who they could trust, but they had to trust someone.

He had hesitated at first, but Roni had insisted that their captain was trustworthy. Less than an hour later, he met them in the South Beach Security penthouse suite, and they laid out all the information they had gathered on Walsh. They also provided him with details about Wilson and Santana, making sure they had covered all the bases about what their investigation had revealed so far.

Rogers glanced between the two of them. "I should read you both the riot act. You for ignoring your medical leave," he said, jabbing a finger in Trey's direction. "And you for not telling me someone tried to kill you," he said, turning his attention to Roni.

"There's more, sir," Roni said and shared a nervous glance with Trey before continuing. "IAD isn't wrong that there's a dirty cop in the department. But we don't think it's Doug."

Rogers narrowed his gaze to peer at them. "I don't get it."

Trey presented the information that Sophie and Rob

had gathered on the monies deposited into Doug's bank accounts and a group of hackers they had managed to identify earlier that day.

Rogers's eyebrows shot up in surprise. "Hackers like those Russian cyberattacks? Or the Chinese? Do you think it's something like that?"

"We're not sure. The hackers could have been working at the direction of someone with the right connections," Roni said.

The captain tilted his head, considering her comments. "Someone like Wilson."

"Possibly, although we're leaning more toward Santana. At a minimum, we think he's providing the locations where the women are being held," Trey explained.

"The Terminal Island site?" Rogers asked.

"It's owned by a shell company and we're trying to find the actual owner," Roni explained.

"We need a warrant to track Walsh's vehicle, plus the usual Sunpass tracking, cell phone data and the rest. We'd also like your help in triangulating the cell phone for my CI who's still missing," Trey said.

"I think I have more than enough to ask for a warrant and I'll get someone to get a fix on your CI's cell phone location, plus all the rest," Rogers said and rose from the dining room table. But as they walked him to the elevators, he said, "You mentioned that there was someone dirty in the department."

Roni hesitated, but then blurted out, "We're leaning toward Ramirez."

"That's a pretty serious charge," the captain said.

"It is and we have nothing to prove it, but we will," Trey said.

With a curt nod, their captain said, "I'll call you as soon as we have more on the cell phone location and the warrant for the tracker."

Once he had gone, they went back to working through all the information they'd gathered so far on Santana and Walsh, but Wilson was still a big black hole in their investigation.

"If he is grabbing women from these parties, would he be so blatant?" Roni posed the question out loud.

Trey shrugged. "Maybe he thinks his money can buy him anything."

"Exactly, so why kidnap women, especially college students? With that much money I'm sure he could find his share of willing partners," Roni said.

Trey had avoided reaching out to Carolina and Mia so far, hoping to keep them out of the investigation, but maybe it was time to ask for their help.

"If anyone knows more about this Wilson guy and what he does at those parties, it's the Twins," he said and dialed Mia.

"*Hola, hermanito.* To what do I owe the pleasure of this call," his sister said facetiously.

"Roni and I need your help in finding out more about John Wilson. I'm putting you on speaker," he said, laying the phone on the table. He hit the speaker button.

"*Hola*, Roni," Mia said, and a second later Carolina piped up with her own hello. "*Hola, amiga.* We hope Trey is treating you well."

Roni looked in his direction and blushed. "He's been the perfect gentleman."

"What a shame," Mia said with a laugh.

Heat flooded his own cheeks and traveled to parts

south as he thought about what he might do with Roni in the very posh and private penthouse, but he fought back that reaction.

"This is all about business," he warned his sister.

"And again, what a shame," Carolina said, making him wonder if the two of them ever had a different thought between them.

"We need your help with John Wilson," Roni said, drawing their attention back to the reason for the call.

With a sigh, Mia said, "What do you need to know besides that he's uber rich, fanatic about his privacy, and probably Miami's most eligible bachelor."

"Seems weird that he's fanatic about his privacy and yet he has these over-the-top penthouse suite parties that end up on social media regularly," Trey said, unable to align the two conflicting ideas.

"Except he's not always at the parties," Carolina explained. "Makes it a big deal when he actually does show up."

Trey shared a look with Roni, and he could see her brain was moving along the same path as his. "And does he leave with anyone when he does show up?"

"Sometimes, but not always. Like I said, he values his privacy," Mia advised.

"Have you guys met him?" Roni asked.

"We have. He's kind of odd," Carolina said.

Trey wished they had video-called the Twins because he could sense there was more they weren't saying and he might have been able to see what it was the Twins were keeping from him.

"Mia. Carolina. You're holding back," he said, pressing them.

"We were invited to go into his private room in the penthouse suite once, but we just got these weird vibes about it, so we made an excuse about having to go to another party. We stopped going to his parties," Mia said, and her discomfort was clear.

Trey cursed under his breath at the thought his sister and cousin might have been in danger, but despite that, he had to ask one more thing.

"Do you think you can get Roni and me into one of those parties?"

"You've been made," he said and let out a stream of curses.

"Not possible. I've been careful," the other man said, but doubt colored his voice.

"Got a call from a friend at the DA who owes me a favor. PD just got a warrant to put a tracker on your car. You need to find other wheels and stay low."

"How can I stay low? We're supposed to be moving the merchandise in four days."

"Merchandise is going to have to wait," he said, thinking that if they couldn't move the women soon, they were going to have to get rid of them. A shame since they were set to bring in an attractive price, but they might not have any choice. The longer they held them, the more risk of discovery. With Gonzalez and Lopez nosing around, they couldn't delay.

"I'll tell the boss," the other man said and hung up.

They had just finished with the Twins when they got a text from Rogers that the warrant had been issued and they'd been able to triangulate the location of Eddie's phone.

Wasting no time, they headed back to the MCP Enterprises building, found Walsh's car in the parking lot and attached the magnetic casing for the GPS tracker beneath the wheel well. Sophie and Rob were going to monitor the GPS feed and update them on any activity.

Armed with the location of Eddie's phone, they headed down *Calle Ocho*, driving through the heart of Little Havana and past the many small shops and restaurants along the avenue. They continued on SW Eighth past the iconic Versailles restaurant and toward the airport. Jets flew overhead while they pushed forward along the Tamiami Trail until they were almost at the start of the Everglades and an uneasy feeling came over Roni.

"This is not good," Trey said, and Roni couldn't disagree.

Turning off SW Eighth, they entered a cul-de-sac of modest but well-kept cinder-block homes. They parked in front of the home where Eddie, or his phone, was supposedly located.

Like the rest of the houses, the home was nicely tended with a palm tree in the center of the yard for shade and colorful crotons and bright annuals in the beds close to the house. Closely clipped grass was damp from the sprinkler system that had wet the lawn and the pavers leading to the front door.

They walked up to the door and knocked. A harried-looking and heavily pregnant woman answered. She was probably in her early forties, with short curly hair and beautiful brown eyes that grew puzzled as they flashed their badges.

"May I help you?" she asked and laid a hand on her swollen belly as if to calm the baby, but before they could answer, the loud shouts of children at play rang out from behind her.

"Kids, be quiet," she shouted and raked back her hair in frustration. "I'm sorry. The boys can be a handful at times."

"We understand. I'm Detective Lopez and this is Detective Gonzalez," Roni said as Trey whipped out his phone and showed the woman a photo of his confidential informant.

"We're looking for this man," he said, but the woman's gaze remained puzzled.

She shook her head and rubbed her belly. "I'm sorry, but he doesn't look familiar."

The ruckus that they'd heard from another room spilled into the space behind her as two boys chased each other into view. They were beating each other with toy trucks and cars, mimicking crash sounds as they did so.

"Boys, *please*! I need to speak to these police officers," the woman shouted and glared at the children, who quieted and lined up behind her.

"The police?" the taller one said, glancing at them with a hint of fear.

His words prompted the younger one to give his brother a shove and say, "See, I told you the cops would come."

The mom whirled on them and jammed her hands on

her hips. "Luis," the mother said, glaring at her youngest. "Why do you think the police would come?"

Luis clasped his hands behind his back and shot a worried look at his brother.

"Luis," the mom pressed, but it was the older boy who answered.

"Because I found a cell phone and kept it," he said. Reaching into his pants pocket, he hauled out a phone and held it out to Roni. She slipped her shirt over her fingers before she grabbed the phone, hoping she could preserve some kind of evidence.

"You've been using it?" Trey asked and dialed Eddie's number.

The phone vibrated in Roni's hand.

"It doesn't have a password," the older brother said and nervously toed the ground with his sneaker.

"Raul Alejandro Garcia. You know better than to keep something that isn't yours," his mother said. She faced them and apologized. "I'm so, so sorry, officers. He didn't mean any harm."

Roni could imagine the thousands of thoughts running through the mother's head, so she tried to de-escalate the situation. "We know he didn't. But we do need his help."

Roni knelt so that she was facing Raul and in a calming voice said, "Raul. Where did you find the phone?"

The boy looked from her to his mother, who nodded for him to continue. In a voice barely above a whisper he said, "By the canal behind the paintball parking lot."

"You know you're not supposed to go by the canal. It's too dangerous," the mom said, her voice wavering between anger and concern.

His small shoulders barely lifted in a shrug. "I didn't

really go near the canal. The phone was by the edge of the parking lot."

"Do you think you could show us where you found it?" Roni asked and the little boy peered at his mom again, as if seeking her permission.

"We'll do whatever you need us to do, officers," the mom said and laid a gentle hand on the boy's shoulder. He visibly relaxed with her touch, confirming to Roni that while he might be getting grounded, that was all that would happen for his misbehavior.

"Great. Can you take us there now, Raul?" Trey asked.

Chapter Eleven

The canal was located behind a small stand of trees and the parking lot for a paintball center. A high chain-link fence separated the parking lot from the trees and canal. A big break in the fence appeared to be well-used based on the trampled grass from the fence to the trees and beyond.

Just past the canal a large swath of wetlands was dotted with sawgrass. The wetlands went for miles, and in the distance, the outlines of mangroves and scrub pines broke up the flatness of the Everglades.

They found Eddie's lower arm at the edge of the canal after the boy gestured in the general direction of where he'd found the phone near the edges of the parking lot. Luckily the boys and their mother had not had to witness that discovery since they'd hung back while Roni and he had slipped through the break in the fence to scope out the area and found the remains.

He'd known it was Eddie from the distinctive tattoo of the Cuban flag inked on the inside of his wrist.

Now he and Roni stood by the edge of the canal, waiting for the divers to hopefully find the rest of his CI.

It seemed like hours while the divers brought up

Eddie's remains bit by bit. As they did so, the medical examiner did her job, cataloging the pieces. They walked over to the ME and her assistant, who was photographing the various parts.

"Any idea on the cause of death or how long he's been in the water?" Trey asked while he examined what the divers had found in the canal.

"Can't decide on COD until we find more of the body. As for how long—there's a lot of predation that's gone on. Alligator and small fish. Based on other skin changes, like this sloughing, a little over a week if I had to guess," the ME said as she slipped Eddie's arm into an evidence bag.

It took him only a second to figure out that Eddie had likely been dead since the night Doug had been murdered.

"We'd appreciate any info you can give us," Roni said and handed the ME her business card.

The ME nodded. "We'll call you as soon as we have anything."

"Thanks," Trey said and slipped a hand behind Roni's back to urge her from the scene.

They were supposed to meet Carolina and Mia in a couple of hours to attend another of Wilson's parties, but in the meantime, there was the issue of Walsh's car.

He started the tracking app that Sophie and Rob had installed on his phone. Much as it had earlier, it showed that Walsh's car was still sitting where it had been for hours.

"No movement," he said and showed Roni the phone. He rubbed the back of his neck, trying to ease the tension growing there. His instincts warned him something was wrong.

Roni shot a quick look at the phone and said, "It's just past five. He's probably still at work."

"Possibly," Trey said, but he didn't have a good feeling about it. "We should head back and see if Sophie and Rob have been able to get anything else for us and get ready to go with Carolina and Mia."

They started to walk back to their car, but as they did so, Roni said, "You're worried someone tipped off Walsh."

With a shrug, he said, "Possibly. But you're probably right that it's just that he's at work. I guess we'll know if it doesn't move soon."

Almost as if on cue, the tracking software chirped and as he looked at the screen, the blip shifted, surprising him. "Looks like you were right," he said and held up the phone.

"Time for us to see where he's going," she said and hurried to the car.

They climbed into the convertible and Trey slipped the phone into a holder so they could monitor the tracking software.

"If he's going home, he'd head either to Seventh or the Dixie Highway to get to Coral Gables," Trey said and used his finger to trace the route he'd take. "It's a short ride. Less than ten minutes."

"Unless he's headed to South Beach. Then he'd shoot over to the causeway, only he's not going either way," Roni said, shaking her head as the blip on the phone unexpectedly moved westward.

"This isn't making any sense," Trey said, watching

as Walsh drove onto SW Twenty-Sixth and moved farther and farther away from the MCP Enterprises building as well as South Beach or his home.

"We have time to try and intercept him," he said, starting the car and driving in the direction of the blip. They were getting closer and closer to Walsh, and he kept his eyes glued to the road, searching for Walsh's vehicle. From the corner of his eye, he could see that Roni was also focused on locating the vehicle. As their path intercepted that of the blip and they started following it, there was still no sign of Walsh's car, a late model Audi.

"I don't get it," Roni said and ran a hand across her forehead, obviously puzzled and frustrated, especially since it seemed they were right on the trail of the car, but it wasn't in sight.

The blip on the tracking software warned that the vehicle was moving off the street they were on and as they watched, a battleship gray Jeep turned off SW 137th and toward the Kendall area. Trey motioned to the Jeep. "Keep an eye on that one," he said, his attention also on whether anyone was trailing them the way they thought they were trailing Walsh.

As the Jeep made a number of turns that matched the activity on the tracking software, it became clear that their GPS tracker was on that vehicle. When they got closer, he could see the car was driven by a middle-aged man with a full dark beard. Barely a few minutes later, the man pulled into the driveway for a large ranch home in West Kendall.

They pulled in across the mouth of the driveway and stepped out, flashing their badges as the man slowly got out of the car and faced them. He raised his hands as if to show he was unarmed, and Trey mimicked the action.

"We just want to ask you a few questions and maybe take a look around the outside of your car," he said.

"I haven't done anything," the man said, hands still raised.

"Sir, you can put your hands down. We know you haven't done anything. As my partner said, we just want to ask a few questions and take a look around, with your permission, of course."

At that the man finally relaxed, stepped away onto his lawn and gestured to his car. "Go ahead and look all you want."

Seeing that Roni had made the man more comfortable, Trey gave her a go-ahead jerk of his head, and she approached the man while he searched the wheel wells of the Jeep.

"We appreciate you're taking the time to chat with us," Roni said and held her hand out for a handshake.

The man eyed her, but then reluctantly shook her hand and said, "Ron Hamilton."

For good measure, she showed him her badge. "I'm Detective Lopez." Pointing at Trey, she said, "That's my partner Detective Gonzalez."

Eyeballing her badge, he did a little shrug and said, "How can I help?"

"Thank you, Mr. Hamilton. Can you tell us where your car was parked today?" she said, watching from the corner of her eye as Trey searched for the tracker.

"In the parking lot for my building. I work for Tradewinds Financial. Our office is in the MCP Enterprises building on Brickell," he said, slowly losing some of his unease.

"Did you lend your car to anyone today or did anyone move it without your knowledge?" she asked, and the man shook his head.

"It was in my spot all day," he said, but his attention was drawn toward the Jeep as Trey moved away from it and toward them.

"Your spot? You have a set spot in the lot?" she pressed.

The man nodded. "All the executives have spots right by the elevators. It's a nice perk when you have to work late at night. Saves you some time, you know."

Trey stood beside her and held out his hand to show her the tracker. Because of that, she knew it was time to wind down their interview.

"Would you mind sharing what spot you were in?" she said, and the man rattled off, "204. Second level and like I said, near the elevator bank."

"We appreciate your help, Mr. Hamilton. We'd also appreciate it if you would not mention this to anyone at this time," Roni said.

When the man seemed surprised by the request, Trey added, "It's just that it's an active investigation and your help would be greatly appreciated."

He handed the man his business card and Roni did the same. "There's no need for you to worry. It's just that your car was in the wrong place at the wrong time."

They walked away and back to their car. As they slipped into the convertible, Trey handed her the GPS tracker. "Someone tipped him off."

Roni shook her head, so violently her hair whipped back and forth across her face. "Not Rogers. I'm sure we can trust him."

With a sharp jerk of his head and a heavy sigh, he said, "I trust your judgment, but if you're right, that means someone at the DA's office is the problem."

She nodded. "It does. We need to let the captain know and we need to check Hamilton's spot to see if there's any CCTV in the area."

"I agree. Let's get going," he said, but as he did so her phone rang.

IAD Detective Ramirez was calling. Her body tensed and she hesitated, unsure of whether or not to answer. Wondering if the timing of the call had anything to do with the discovery of Eddie's remains and the wild-goose chase they'd just taken thanks to the GPS tracker.

"Aren't you going to answer?" Trey asked and motioned to the phone.

She swiped to ignore the call. "It's Ramirez, but I don't want to talk to him."

Trey turned his attention back to the roadway, hands clenched on the steering wheel.

"What does Ramirez want with you?" he asked and shot a quick look in her direction.

She shrugged and said, "Don't know and don't care."

He grunted, as if accepting the explanation, but she sensed the tension in his body, warning her that he hadn't necessarily bought what she'd said.

No matter. Even though the lie was bitter on her tongue, she was going to have to lie to him again until the time was right to tell him about her involvement with IAD.

THE FRANTIC CALL from his connection at the district attorney's office had come in just as he was leaving to meet his ex-wife for dinner. Her constant demands for support money were the reason that he'd been forced to do some favors that had turned into way more than he'd ever expected or wanted.

As he'd heard the woman's worried recounting of how the DA had been calling in staff about the leak of the warrant information, he knew he had no choice about what to do.

He'd somehow talked her off the ledge and agreed to meet her.

He'd also blown off dinner with his ex-wife, earning him a very nasty attack and threat to call her lawyer, but that was the least of his problems.

His anger at having to deal with yet another issue grew to where he almost felt as if his head would explode. Hands shaking, he dialed Walsh, pretty sure of what the idiot had done, but he had to confirm it for himself.

Walsh answered. "I wasn't expecting your call. I thought I was supposed to lie low."

"Did you move the GPS tracker?" he asked, his body vibrating with anger.

"Yeah, I did. I wish I could have seen their faces when they realized they were chasing the wrong person," Walsh said with a laugh.

"You've just blown my contact at the DA's. You should have left it on the car and taken a different one like I instructed."

Dead silence greeted his rebuke.

"I thought I was helping," Walsh replied, sounding

like a repentant child, which only upped his anger at Santana for thinking Walsh would make a good addition to their team.

"Don't help. You've only made things worse," he said and was about to hang up when Walsh said, "What should I do now?"

A million thoughts, nasty ones at that, rushed through his brain, but he gritted his teeth and said, "Nothing. Just sit your ass at home until I can figure out what to do."

He hung up then, but his mind continued racing as worry bit deep.

Another loose end he had to deal with. Two if he included Walsh.

Add to that Adams and the woman who had died unexpectedly.

Too many bodies, but he had no doubt there would soon be more, including Lopez. Maybe even Gonzalez. He'd never liked the cocky detective who got treated like royalty because of his family's connections.

Although Lopez hadn't said anything to incriminate him so far, he'd seen her that night at the club. He had no doubt she'd seen Adams and Walsh. He was afraid that she'd seen him as well, not that she had mentioned it.

Shaking his head, he went to his car and looked around before reaching into his glove compartment. He took out the throwaway gun. It already had a number of bodies on it from his various jobs for the boss.

What was a few more?

"WE REALLY OWE you big-time," Trey said as Sophie and Rob joined them at the dining room table.

"You're *familia*, Trey. It's what family does for family," Rob said, flipping open his laptop.

Familia. It reminded him of what Roni had said to him the day of the funeral—that she would help him because he was family. But it seemed that everyone was going above and beyond for him. It brought guilt that for way too many years he'd been pushing away from them, or rather, from the family business. But here they were for him, using all the resources of that business to help him and Roni.

"I really appreciate it. I'm not sure I really deserve it," he said, the guilt weighing heavily on him.

Sophie rolled her eyes. She walked over to Roni and wrapped an arm around her shoulders. "We're doing it for Roni, too, *primo*. She's like family as well."

Roni smiled and the faintest hint of pink swept across her cheeks. "I appreciate that, Sophie."

"I think you'll appreciate everything we've found for you so far," Rob said and with a few taps of the keyboard, projected his screen to the monitor.

"We weren't able to break through the corporate shell on the Terminal Island property. But we were able to find out that the attorney who incorporated that company did two others at the same time. The ultimate owner of those two other properties was MCP Enterprises," Rob said, excitement ringing in his tone.

"Sounds like a visit to that attorney is in order," Roni said.

With a nod, Sophie continued with their report and blasted a different image onto the large monitor. "We were also able to break into the CCTV feed for the parking lot. Watch the spot you told us about."

Trey focused on the grainy video, but despite the low quality of the black-and-white video, there was no doubt who walked by the gray Jeep and slipped a hand beneath the back wheel well. It was exactly where he'd found their GPS tracker on the Jeep.

"That's Walsh," Roni said.

"It is. Unfortunately, we can't use this video to prove anything. But there's no way he found that tracker on his own. Someone had to tell him," Trey warned again, frustrated that it seemed that someone was always one step ahead of them. He worried that one of those steps could bring harm to Roni or one of his family members.

"Captain Rogers is coordinating with the DA's office, who's doing their own investigation," Roni advised and reached out to lay a hand on his, offering reassurance.

The ding of the elevator warned that they had company, making him shoot to his feet with concern, but as the doors opened, Carolina and Mia spilled out, carrying an assortment of bags again. This time some large garment bags as well as bags from one of the better-known Asian fusion restaurants in the area.

Smiling, Mia waved one restaurant bag up in the air and said, "Dinner! We thought you'd need to eat before we headed to Del Sol tonight."

"I'll take these into Roni's room," Carolina said and rushed off with the garment bags.

Trey tamped down his frustration at the interruption but reined it in since he knew the Twins were only trying to be helpful and keep things chill. Biting his lip, he said, "We appreciate it, but we have just a couple of things to finish up."

He glanced at Sophie and Robbie, who nodded in unison.

"Just one thing, really, but we can move over to let the Twins put out their spread," Sophie said. She grabbed her laptop and shifted to the sitting area, placing her computer on a coffee table.

Roni took hold of his hand and tugged him in the direction of the sofa while Rob joined Carolina and Mia in setting the table and opening the take-out dishes.

The aromas of the food wafted over as Sophie showed Roni and him what else they'd been able to find out about the bank deposits. "Like we told you the other day, there was something totally off with how the monies got into the accounts. It appears that Doug's bank reported a possible cyberattack in the days after his death. The attack was immediately after Doug was killed. Rob and I think they did that in order to be able to access Doug's accounts and change the information for the deposits."

Trey held his hands up to slow her down. "But the money came from a real account?"

Sophie nodded. "It did the same way anyone would do a wire transfer using the right bank codes and account numbers. We think they got Doug's account number and access to manipulate the data with a cyberattack, especially now that the bank is publicly reporting that they might have had an issue."

"But you have no idea who was behind it?" Roni chimed in from beside him.

Sophie shook her head. "Just like any crime scene, someone may leave fingerprints behind but with this, it'll take a lot more time to pinpoint who may be responsible. I think that with the information we've gotten, you'll be able to get a warrant for information on the owner of that Swiss account."

Trey nodded, smiled and hugged his cousin. "*Gracias.* You've done an amazing job. As soon as we have some faith in who we can trust at the DA, we'll work with them to get that warrant. Can you send this information to me?"

"We can, and we'll keep on digging to see if we can find those digital fingerprints for you," she said, before she shut down the laptop and stood.

"Any chance those fingerprints could lead to John Wilson?" Roni asked, rising from the sofa as well and walking with Sophie toward the dining table.

Sophie shrugged and did a little wag of her head, sending strands of her dark shoulder-length hair shifting against the strong line of her jaw—a determined jaw. Trey knew his cousin would keep on digging.

"Anything is possible," Sophie said.

As THEY REACHED the table, Roni realized that Carolina and Mia had been extravagant with the dinner, the way they went overboard with most everything else they did. Of course, maybe that's what had propelled them into being top influencers. Their lifestyle blog and social media accounts not only opened doors throughout Miami for them, they'd made her friends millionaires by their midtwenties.

Dishes from a well-known Chinese/Japanese restaurant covered the table. At least four different kinds of dim sum. Assorted sushi, sashimi and crispy rolls.

For the main dishes—Peking duck, shrimp tempura, a large rib eye steak and a trio of noodles and rice dishes.

"Do you plan on feeding an army?" Roni asked jokingly, but the words had no sooner left her mouth when the elevator dinged to announce they had visitors.

It was impossible for her to miss how Trey's body tensed up as his mother, father and younger brother Ricky walked off the elevator, also carrying an assortment of bags. "We brought dessert," Samantha Gonzalez said in a way that made Roni immediately think of her best friend Mia. The apple had clearly not fallen far from the tree.

The same was true for the men of the family as a stern-faced *Ramoncito* Gonzalez faced his equally stoic son.

"Papi," Trey said, as he bro-hugged his father and accepted an exuberant hug and kiss from his mother.

"Mom. So good to see you," he said, which earned a short laugh from his mother.

"I can tell from your happy face," she teased and stroked a hand across Trey's cheek.

Ricky hugged Roni and then fist-bumped his brother. "You never let me know when to come chat with you," he said.

"Not quite ready for you yet," Trey said.

"Or ever," Ricky said and chuckled.

Roni couldn't bite back her own laugh at the admonitions from his family, and accepted hugs from Trey's parents, whom she truly loved. She'd known them since she'd started going to high school with Mia and Carolina. They'd always been warm and welcoming.

But having a big family dinner while in the midst

of an investigation wasn't typical, not that anything about the Gonzalez family was typical. From their escape from Cuba to their rise to become one of Miami's more prominent Cuban American families, the Gonzalez family was unique.

Trey's mother motioned to the table and said, "It's been so long since we all got together, we thought we'd take advantage—"

"Of our enforced captivity?" Trey said with a lift of a brow.

"Considering you've been all over, it's not really captivity, is it?" Carolina challenged with her own arch of a perfectly manicured brow.

"Touché, *prima*," Trey said with a stiff smile.

They were about to sit when Roni's phone rang. Heath was calling.

"You'll have to excuse me for a moment," she said and walked away to chat with him.

"Heath. Thanks for the info you sent on the hotel staff," she said although they hadn't had a chance to delve into it. Trey and she hoped to check out the list of Del Sol names before they went there tonight.

"I did some research on Wilson, but I'm sure you already know he's like a big deal in the tech world," Heath said, a hint of annoyance in his voice.

"I did. We're trying to get into one of his parties tonight," she admitted, feeling guilty that she hadn't shared more with her partner right off the bat.

"Rough life, Roni. By the way, Ramirez came by again to ask where you were. I stonewalled him, but I don't know how long I can hold him off before he gets too suspicious," he said.

Her radar was once again saying that she could trust her new partner, but not the IAD detective. "You need to watch yourself around Ramirez."

"You think he's involved with all that's going down?" Heath said, but his tone was hushed, barely audible, thanks to the background noise in the squad room.

"I do. Say nothing to anyone besides the captain. I'll keep you posted in the morning on what happens tonight so we can plan our next steps," she said.

"Roger that, Roni. Stay safe," he said and hung up.

She walked back to the table where the Gonzalez family had left her a spot next to Trey, of course. The Twins and possibly everyone else was matchmaking to her chagrin, not that she'd let them know it was getting to her.

Nor to Trey, who was also playing it cool in front of his family.

But as the food was passed around and plates were filled, Trey leaned close to her and asked, "Everything okay?"

She nodded. "It was Heath with some info. Ramirez came looking for me again."

Chapter Twelve

It bothered Trey that Ramirez seemed to have so much interest in Roni. Too much interest and he worried there was more that Roni wasn't telling him about her relationship with the IAD detective.

With a dip of his head, he said, "I know he probably questioned you about that night, only… Is there something else you want to tell me, Roni?"

Her body jumped beside his and she hesitantly met his gaze. Vehemently shaking her head, hair swishing around that determined jaw, she said, "What do you mean?"

"You know what I mean. Did IAD want more than just some answers from you?" he pushed.

"*Mi' jo*, it's not time for work," his mother admonished, clearly picking up on the tense vibes between them.

Since all of his family grew quiet and looked his way, he opted to drop the subject. For now. When they were alone later, he intended to get to the bottom of whatever was happening with Roni and IAD.

"I'm sorry," he said. "It is time for family and not work." From beside him came Roni's relieved sigh and the escape of tension from her body.

He filled his belly with the wonderful food his family had brought, giving into hunger as he realized that they hadn't eaten all day. As his hunger was sated, he realized that his family's company, their unqualified love and support, was also providing a balm to the pain and anger that had been in his heart since his partner's death.

When his mother and sister got up to make coffee and bring out the dessert, he helped Roni, Sophie and Carolina clear off the table and put away any leftovers. Ricky and Rob joined them a second later with the last of the dishes.

As he sidled up to Trey to help, Ricky said, "I'm serious about that chat, Trey. You've had a lot happen lately. You're not yourself."

"I appreciate the offer, but not right now, Ricky," he said as he snapped the lid on one of the containers and reached for another.

His brother clapped him on the back, but kept quiet, aware that he wasn't going to change Trey's mind now. Maybe never, not that Ricky would stop trying.

If there was one thing Trey knew, his family would always have his back. But would Roni?

He shot a quick look at his watch, worried about the time, but it was barely seven and South Beach nightlife didn't get going until much later.

"Don't worry, *hermano*. Party doesn't start until nine," Mia said as she caught him checking his watch.

He should have been relieved by that, except that he was eager to move on the investigation of Wilson. He also resolved to get Roni alone and grill her about what was happening with the IAD detectives.

But for now, that would have to wait in favor of the table laden with coffees, sweet Cuban flan, and *pastelitos*.

He forced himself to sit and plaster on a smile, but that smile grew more natural as his family's love worked its magic. Or maybe it was the sweetness of the flan, he told himself, avoiding the thought that it seemed totally natural to have Roni beside him and part of his family.

Natural unless he thought about the fact that he worried she was keeping something from him.

As the group finished up dessert, Mia and Carolina excused themselves and dragged Roni away so that they could get dressed for Wilson's party.

"That's our cue to go," Sophie said.

Rob nodded and said, "Hopefully we'll have more for you soon."

Trey clapped Rob on the back. "We appreciate all you're doing."

"I'll head out also," Ricky said and followed his cousins to the elevator bank, leaving Trey alone with his mother and father.

He braced himself for the usual guilt trip. To head it off, he said, "I appreciate all the resources that SBS has put to our disposal."

His father didn't say anything at first. He just pulled his shoulders back and jammed his hands into his pockets. But then his mother elbowed him, and his father said, "You are family, Trey. You and Roni. We will do anything we can to keep you both safe."

Safe being something his family regularly worried about. It was impossible to ignore those concerns given what had happened barely over a week earlier. But he tried. "You don't have to worry about us."

His father sucked in a quick breath and appeared ready to lash out at him, but another sharp poke from his mother seemed to drive the air from him.

"We do worry, Ramon. Still, we trust you and Roni to make the right decisions," his mother said, jumping in as she often did to avoid conflict between the two men.

"*Gracias, mami.* We *will* take care and we do appreciate everything you've done for us," he said and reached out to hug his mom. After, he offered his hand to his father, who reluctantly shook it.

Satisfied things were under control, his mother slipped her arm through his father's. "Time for us to go, *Ramoncito.* Trey has things to do."

With a gruff harrumph, his father let himself be tugged to the elevators and out of the room.

A blast of laughter, Carolina and Mia's, drifted from behind the closed doors of the bedroom Roni was using, warning him that he still had to face the Twins and their matchmaking.

Definitely time to get his head ready for tonight's assignment.

"*Mira, chicas.* I so appreciate what you're trying to do, but me and Trey—"

"Would be perfect together, but that's not what this dress is about, Roni," Mia said as she held the dress in front of her body and swayed back and forth in front of the mirror.

Roni flinched at the lack of fabric in the dress. Mia and she were of a like height and based on what she was seeing, the dress would only reach midthigh. Then there was the low-cut bodice as well as cutouts at strategic locations that revealed a great deal of skin.

"It's about attracting Wilson since he'll be there. If you catch his assistant's attention, you may get into Wilson's private suite," Carolina explained.

"And what happens then?" Roni asked and her friends shared a look.

With a quick lift of her shoulders, Mia said, "We're told that you and another half a dozen or so women sit around and drink while His Majesty decides who will play video games with him."

"Seriously?" Roni asked, totally surprised. At her friends' nods, she said, "That's it?"

"Apparently if you're the last one standing, Wilson may ask you to stay the night. Or at least that's what we've heard," Carolina said.

"Why didn't you mention this before?" Roni wondered as she accepted the dress that Mia handed her, even though she dreaded donning it.

"They seemed like idle rumors, and we wanted to confirm them before we told you," Mia said.

"Were you able to do that?" she asked and toed off her flat-heeled shoes, earning a disgusted look from Carolina. "Do you have to wear those when you work?"

Roni rolled her eyes and shucked off her socks. "You try running after a suspect in three-inch heels," she said although she suspected her friends would somehow manage to do it.

That they also thought they could was reinforced by their hearty chuckles and the look they shared.

She walked to the bed, rummaged through a bag and whipped something out that she tossed to Roni.

Snagging the tiny scrap of fabric midair, she held it up and winced at its size. Biting her lip because she had a job to do and this was part of the job, she peeled off her own panties and slipped on the barely-there thong. Her bra joined her panties on the floor and a second later Mia was helping her slip on the dress.

It went on as snug as a second skin and it took a few tugs and smoothing in a final adjustment.

"Let's hope we can find out more today," Roni said and accepted the high heels Mia passed her way, grateful they'd kept them to a reasonable height.

"Let's, but first, hair and makeup," Carolina said with a snap of her fingers.

Grimacing, Roni relented and followed Trey's cousin into the bathroom.

TREY GRITTED HIS teeth as he watched their possible suspect eyeballing Carolina, Mia and Roni. *What straight sane man wouldn't?* he thought.

The Twins always attracted action. They were beautiful women and confident. The locals also knew they were successful and sought-after for all the top events in Miami. Being with the Twins opened doors and that made them quite a catch. And with Carolina and Mia's tutelage, Roni was the proverbial butterfly emerging from a cocoon.

She was stunning. They'd done her shoulder-length hair up in a casual topknot that had the kind of look that said she might have just put it up after a night of sex.

Smoky makeup highlighted her eyes, drawing out

the gold shot through the hazel. Eyeliner accented a slightly exotic tilt he'd never noticed before.

He couldn't pay too much attention to the revealing dress his sister and cousin had chosen for Roni or he'd go crazy. There was a sheer triangular panel across her midsection that displayed her toned abs and made him want to walk over and slide his hands all over her lean body.

A man stepped in front of Roni, blocking his view with his silk-suited back.

It's on, he thought and focused his attention on the Twins and Roni. The man appeared animated, smiling and gesticulating as he chatted with them.

As they'd discussed, they were supposed to play it a little coy, especially since Roni had rebuffed him when he'd made the overture the other night. If it even occurred to him that this was the same woman since Roni looked so different compared to their last visit.

The Twins and Roni chatted for a few more minutes with the man gesturing back toward the lobby. Mia, Carolina and Roni seemed to be discussing his invitation, but then Mia shot to her feet and smiled at the man as if to seal the invitation.

Their possible suspect held his hand out for the women to precede him.

That was Trey's cue to intercept them. He hurried from his spot at the bar and rushed to the front door, arriving there just as the quartet did.

"Trey," Mia called out and rushed over. She rose on tiptoe and brushed a kiss on his cheek and turned to introduce him to the man.

"Miles, this is my brother Trey. *Hermano*, I didn't

realize you'd be here tonight," she said, laying it on thickly.

"I hope I'm not interrupting," he said pointedly. He walked over to kiss Carolina and Roni and shook the man's hand. "Nice to meet you."

The man appeared suddenly uneasy. "We should get going," he said and gestured in the direction of the elevators.

"We should. Why don't you join us, Trey?" Carolina said, as planned.

"I'd love to. *Gracias*," he said and slipped behind Roni to lay a hand at the small of her back, the movement almost instinctive. Definitely possessive.

Miles didn't fail to notice the action, forcing Trey to quickly pull away and offer the man a wry smile, as if to say, "Don't fault me for trying."

"It is okay for my brother Trey to join us, isn't it?" Mia said, clearly forcing Miles's hand.

With a nod, Miles acquiesced and called the elevator. When it arrived and they boarded, he used a key card to unlock passage to the penthouse suite.

The ride up the twenty-something stories was smooth. When the elevator opened into the suite, they strolled out into an area about the size of half a city block. Floor-to-ceiling windows along the front of the room led to a terrace with views of the beachfront and the pool below. From the windows on either side of the room he could see the neighboring hotels, beaches, and in the distance, the city of Miami.

The room was packed with beautiful women lounging at low-slung couches or at chairs and tables on the terrace outside. As he stepped farther into the room, he noticed a bar tucked away in a corner where a bartender was handing out drinks while two other servers walked around with beverages and assorted canapés. When the elevator opened behind them again, two more servers exited with fresh trays of food and walked around the room and onto the terrace.

Electronic dance music pumped out of speakers and melded with the sounds of conversation and laughter from the women gathered there.

It hit Trey then. Besides Miles and him, there were no other men. Even the bartender and servers were all women.

"Make yourselves at home," Miles said with a sweep of his hand and before any of them could react, he hurried around the corner.

Trey tried to follow surreptitiously and observed as Miles slipped through a door to another room.

Wilson's private suite, he thought and wondered whether he should have stayed back to improve the chances of Roni, Carolina and Mia getting into the suite. But he'd had to see for himself what was happening. At first glance it looked like the kind of extravagant event regularly held by the celebrities who flocked to South Beach for just this kind of nightlife. Except that men were clearly not welcome, making him wonder why.

He inched back toward the women, stood next to Roni and whispered, "I'm going to nose around and try to ask some questions, but then I think it would be best if I left."

Roni nodded and laid a hand on his chest. "We can handle this."

He had to trust that they could take care of themselves and forced himself to leave them by the bar, where he hoped Miles would see that they were now alone.

As he walked around, he smiled at the various women, chatting and indulging them when they asked for a selfie as if he was someone special, possibly because he was the only man there. He took selfies as well, hoping he wouldn't have to use them to identify anyone who went missing or worse.

After about an hour, he strolled across the terrace and back inside. Standing by the elevators, he snapped a panorama shot and as the elevator opened with more servers carrying food, he got in, telling himself not to worry about those he was leaving behind.

"THANK YOU FOR meeting with me," the woman said, her gaze darting nervously around the interior of the nearly empty café where he'd asked her to meet him.

"Of course, Sylvia. Can I get you a *café con leche*?" he asked, faking concern. He'd gotten good at that over the years, and it had come in quite handy more than once.

"*Sí, gracias,*" she said while wringing her hands and continuing to scan the room.

He walked to the counter and ordered two coffees. Once they arrived, he handed the server the money and the young man walked away to make change. With his back to Sylvia to block her view, he dropped a roofie into one cup, turned and walked with the coffees to their table.

He placed the tainted coffee in front of her, sat and

took a sip of his. Grimacing, he said, "Bitter. You might want more sugar."

She reacted as he wanted, adding a couple of spoons of sugar and stirring. The extra sugar would hopefully mask any aftertaste from the roofie.

"The DA wanted to speak to me, but I left before they could track me down," she said and finally sipped the coffee.

"You didn't have to do that. You didn't do anything wrong," he said, trying to put her at ease until the roofie kicked in.

"But I told you about the warrant," she said, her hands shaking as she raised the coffee cup for another sip.

"I'm a cop. We're the ones executing the warrant," he said calmly and watched as Sylvia's eyes slowly grew unfocused.

"Are you okay?" he asked and placed a hand on her arm to steady her as she wavered in her seat.

"I'm not feeling too well," she said, her words slightly slurred.

He rose, slipped an arm around her, and helped her to her feet. "Let me take you home."

He'd parked right in front of the building, having planned for this. In front for a quick getaway, but out of view of the CCTV cameras in the area.

Her knees started to give out, forcing him to tighten his hold on her as he opened his car door and unceremoniously dumped her in the front seat. He shut the door, uncaring that it slammed her head, and hurried around to the driver's side.

It pleased him to see that Sylvia's body had slumped

below the edge of the window. No one looking at the car would think anyone was with him. Likewise, if he passed any CCTV cameras, it would look like there was only the driver in the car.

He turned on the car radio and drove, singing along and tapping the steering wheel to the beats of the Latin music as he did so. But as he neared the spot where he'd left Eddie, he realized there was a police vehicle there along with a mobile forensic laboratory.

Cursing under his breath, he pushed deeper into the Everglades, both annoyed and worried.

If they'd already found Eddie, it might mean that Gonzalez and Lopez were getting closer than he wanted. With only a few days left to either move the women or eliminate them, he was going to have to decide what to do.

Chapter Thirteen

It had been well over an hour since they'd arrived, and Miles had gone into the other room.

In all that time Trey had been strolling around, seemingly snapping selfies, but she knew he had been scoping out what was happening and who was there just in case. Hopefully they wouldn't have to use any of the selfies to identify anyone.

She had also been keeping an eye on things, but so far nothing made her radar zing. Except for Miles's activities and his prolonged absence into the room where she assumed Wilson was residing.

To her surprise, when the door opened it wasn't Miles who came out, but another man. Wilson, she assumed.

She'd seen photos of him on the internet and thought he was an average-looking guy, but in person he was way more attractive. Unlike Miles with his slick bespoke suit, Wilson was dressed casually in a white linen *guayabera*. The two rows of pleats running down the front of the shirt emphasized his broad chest and flat stomach. *No gaming flab there*, she thought.

He wore matching linen pants and leather flip-flops,

and as he stepped out, he walked with his hands out-stretched, as if he was a messiah blessing his followers.

Mia, who was standing behind her, whispered into her ear, "That's him."

She leaned back slightly to murmur, "Seems full of himself."

"Out here. When he's inside his private sanctuary not so much we heard," Carolina muttered.

Interesting, Roni thought.

She kept her eyes on him, watching as he did his benediction walk and the women responded, touching him or his clothes. Smiling at him, their looks between reverent and calculating. There were definitely women here to see if they could snag the wealthy tech millionaire.

The whole time he strolled around Wilson was smiling, but the smile didn't reach up into his eyes. As his gaze happened to connect with hers for the briefest second, it was assessing.

Is he choosing his next victim? she thought and forced herself to sip her drink and seem at ease, but her radar was now pinging major league. There was something off about this man, but did it mean he was a kidnapper and a murderer?

Wilson chose a group of women on the terrace to grace with his presence, lingering there to chat with them. Apparently saying something funny as the women all started laughing, but the laughter struck her as being as fake as their boobs and bee-stung lips.

"How do you *chicas* do this all the time?" she wondered aloud. Her friends might be fashionable and popular, but she'd never known them to be phony.

With a shrug, Mia said, "It's a job."

She realized then that she'd never really talked to her friends about what had made them start their lifestyle blog and if they were happy with where it had gone. Especially with Mia's response and Carolina's blasé shrug echoing Mia's sentiment.

She intended to change that and be a better friend once this investigation was done.

Dragging her mind back to the investigation, she caught sight of Wilson waving at the women and walking away from the group of giggling sycophants. He backtracked into the suite, weaving through the crowd of women. He paused occasionally to grace someone with a smile and a touch and then he was heading back in their direction.

He stopped in front of them and dipped his head. "Mia. Carolina. So nice of you to come to my party. Who's your friend?"

Roni held out her hand and gave the name she used while undercover. "Sarita Mendez."

Wilson peered at her hand for a hot second, clearly uneasy, but then he took hold of it in both of his and gave it an almost priestly squeeze. "Sarita. Beautiful name for a beautiful woman."

Lame, she thought, but forced a smile and thanked him. "I appreciate that, John. May I call you John?"

"Of course. Would you like to join me for a drink? Just you." He gazed past her to the Twins and said, "I'm not in the mood to see my face in your posts again."

Mia shook her head, but said, "Go ahead, Sarita. We were going to head to another party anyway."

Mia and Carolina hugged her and walked away, but

they weren't headed to another party. They'd agreed that if Wilson selected only one of them, the others would advise Trey so he could stay in contact. But the fact that Wilson had recognized the Twins and had still invited her to go with him, knowing full well that they would be aware of that, lessened her worry about going off alone with him.

Not that a true psychopath would worry in that situation. They would likely think they could talk their way out of anything. Hadn't Dahmer and Bundy?

Wilson waved a hand in invitation as Miles opened the door to his private area. As she walked toward the door, Wilson swept his hand down her back. His touch was slightly cold and sent a shiver through her.

The front wall of the private suite had floor-to-ceiling windows that faced Ocean Drive and the city beyond. A large bed was tucked against one wall while a huge sofa faced a collection of monitors on the other.

"Please join me," he said and gestured not toward the bed, but to the sofa.

She did, sitting beside him on the comfy cushions. On the table before them were an assortment of snacks and candies. An ice bucket held not wine, but sodas.

Weird, she thought, but a second later it got even weirder as Wilson held out a game controller to her.

The word erupted from her before she could control it. "Seriously?"

She muttered a curse and winced that she might have blown the assignment with that unguarded reaction.

To her surprise, Wilson laughed and thrust the controller at her again. "Seriously. I could tell you weren't fake, Sarita. That's why I chose you. And you have good hands."

His comment puzzled her, but as she took hold of the controller, she realized her hands were the one thing they hadn't done up. Her nails were neatly trimmed with only a simple clear polish. She wore only one small ring on her index finger and a thin gold bracelet at her wrist.

"*Gracias*, I think." *What did someone say to a compliment like that?*

"Have you ever played before?" he said with a flip of his hand at the wall of monitors that jumped to life to display a simulation of a city that had suffered apocalyptic destruction.

"I've played it with a younger brother," she said and that seemed enough for Wilson, who clicked a button on the controller and started the game.

Despite her surprise, she immediately engaged, sensing that it was important to Wilson. Hoping that once they finished the game, the evening would play out as she had expected, namely, with Wilson making a sexual advance.

But once they successfully navigated one level after another, it seemed there would be no end to the game. During their play, Wilson would occasionally lean forward to stick his hand in one of the bowls of chips, pretzels and candies, stuffing them into his face. He snagged a soda from the bucket and sucked it down, all while still managing to push the buttons on the controller.

"Damn, you're good," he said with a whoop as she blasted one zombie as it came at them. It was a lot easier to do than the shooting tests she regularly had to take for the police force or the real-life situations when she'd had to consider using her weapon.

"*Gracias,*" she said and continued eliminating zombies, vampires and other dangers until Wilson finally, and apparently reluctantly, paused the game.

He swiveled on the couch to face her. "Thanks for playing with me," he said and motioned for Miles to come over.

She hadn't even realized that the man had slipped back into the room—she'd been so occupied with playing the game and trying to get a handle on Wilson, who had gone from that almost savior-like figure and playboy to a teenage, basement-dwelling gamer.

She shook her head in disbelief as Miles handed her a card. It had only one line on it: a phone number. "I don't get it, John."

Wilson did a casual dip of his head. "You're not fake, Sarita. And you're a darn good gamer." He ducked his head down and like an uncertain teenager, he said, "Beautiful. You're welcome to come back whenever you want."

She looked at Miles, who smiled a real smile and not the bogus one she'd seen on other occasions. His eyes had lost their deadness and were now alight with pleasure. "We mean it, Sarita. You can't imagine how hard it is for John to find someone real. I'm his half brother, by the way."

Blowing out a harsh laugh, she said, "Maybe you're looking in all the wrong places and at all the wrong people."

"You mean I should like all the right people like your

friends Mia and Carolina?" Wilson said, but surprisingly it wasn't a challenging statement.

She considered how her friends would treat him if he stepped out of this totally fabricated facade and nodded. "*Sí*, like Mia and Caro. They're real people," she replied.

"I think you know how to reach them," she added, and rose from the sofa and walked toward the door. But she paused there, turned and held up the card Miles had given her. "Thanks for a fun night. I will call."

She wanted to keep an open line to him just in case there was more to this bizarre night that she wasn't seeing.

She rode the elevators to the lobby and strolled out onto the steps of the hotel. She looked around and realized that Trey was sitting off to one side of the wide veranda at the front of the hotel.

He sauntered to her and laid a hand at her waist. "Are you okay?"

"I am," she said, and they walked toward the valet at the curb.

"Mia and Carolina said Wilson took you into his private room. What happened in there?" he asked, searching her features for any sign of upset.

"You're not going to believe me when I tell you." She displayed the card with the phone number and said, "He wanted a gaming partner."

Trey examined the card as they reached the curb. A valet rushed up to them and he passed the man the ticket for the convertible. The young man sprinted away to get their car.

"I don't get it," Trey said and returned the card.

"We played a video game. All night. And it turns out Miles is his half brother."

Trey shook his head. "The weird feeling Mia and Carolina got was—"

"Off, but not in a way we should worry about. I mean, it is weird, but aren't there a lot of eccentric millionaires?" she said with a quick wobble of her head.

Trey cursed, but just then a car turned the corner with the screech of tires on the pavement and veered into the wrong lane of traffic in front of the hotel. The dark muzzle of a gun poked from the driver's-side window.

"Get down," Trey screamed and hauled her to the ground behind a parked car, covering her body with his as a spray of gunfire pinged against vehicles and shattered glass.

After the gunfire had ended, he helped her sit up. "You okay?"

"I'm okay," she said, even though there was a burning sensation along her right arm.

Trey muttered a curse. "You're hit."

There was only a small graze on her upper arm. "I'm okay," she said and accepted his help to get to her feet. She wobbled on the high heels, but he steadied her.

"Are you sure?" he asked even as a police car jerked to a halt in front of the hotel, lights flashing, casting eerie red and blue lights that battled with the neon from the buildings along the strip. A second cruiser arrived a second later and the officers streamed from their vehicles to check on those who had been on the sidewalk when the shooting started.

Trey and Roni did the same. Trey pulled his badge

out from his pocket and Roni slipped her hand beneath the hem of the dress to the holder wrapped high around her thigh. They showed the badges to the officers and civilians they helped.

Luckily no pedestrians or hotel patrons had been shot, and there were only minor injuries from people diving out of the way to avoid the gunfire. The EMTs tended to them and Roni. After, Trey and Roni worked with the other officers to take down names and get as many firsthand accounts as they could about the car and shooter.

Captain Rogers arrived in a squad car just as they were heading into the hotel to request the videos from their security cameras. "Lopez. Gonzalez. Do you have any idea if this was related to your investigation?"

Sadly, there had been a number of shootings on Ocean Drive and nearby areas. "It's possible, but we can't say for sure," she said.

Rogers gestured to her arm, which had been bandaged by one of the EMTs "Are you okay?"

She nodded. "I'm fine and we have witness accounts of the car and driver as well as our own observations."

"Good. Let's go see what those security videos have for us," Rogers said.

Chapter Fourteen

The adrenaline was wearing off as they returned to the penthouse.

Trey's hand shook as he reached out to take Roni's uninjured arm and applied gentle pressure to urge her to face him.

She did, her muscles trembling beneath his hand as she finally released her grasp on the control she'd exerted at the crime scene. Lifting her gaze, she met his and the invitation there was clear.

He might have lost her tonight. Might have died himself. He wasn't going to refuse her. He wasn't going to hold back.

He hauled her close and kissed her, meeting her mouth over and over again as she strained against him.

He moaned, needing her more than he needed breath. Needing to make love to her to remind both of them that they were very much alive. That it was time they stopped denying what they felt for each other.

Still kissing, arms wrapped around each other, he backed her up until they were lying on the large couch in the middle of the room. Her body all soft womanly curves against his, but he worried he was too heavy on her. Shifting slowly, he let her be on top and in control because he had to know she wanted this as much as he did.

She slipped over his hips, her dress hiked up almost to her waist, and cradled his erection at her center. She leaned her arms on his chest, mindful of his injured shoulder. "I want this," she said as if reading his mind and with no hesitation, she reached down and whipped the dress up and over her head.

Dios, she was gorgeous, he thought at the sight of her beautiful breasts. He cupped them and they fit into his big hands perfectly. Pushing up on one arm, he ignored the twinge of pain in his side to kiss her pebbled nipples.

A WASH OF heat and wet erupted at her core at the first touch of his mouth on her. At the sight of him, his dark hair against her fairer skin, her heart raced in her chest.

She cupped his head to her with one hand while fumbling with the buttons on his shirt with the other. Frustrated, she finally jerked the shirt loose, sending buttons flying to ping on the glass of the nearby coffee table.

They both chuckled at that and Trey arched a brow. "Impatient?" he teased.

"Sí," she said and laid her hands on his chest, running them across the taut muscles and a light trail of hair. The evidence of his injuries, still raw and angry, was a jolt to her system. A reminder of how she might have lost him without ever experiencing this.

She bent to kiss him again while she moved her

hands on him, tracing the muscles of his chest and lower. There was no fumbling as she undid the button on his pants and drew down the zipper. Freed him as he shimmied to escape his pants and underwear.

He was large in her hands. Thick. And she trembled at the thought of him inside her.

"Condom," she said in an urgent whisper, and he whispered, "Wallet."

She snatched his pants off the floor, found the wallet and condom, but didn't rush as she caressed him before deliberately rolling the condom into place.

"You're killing me," he said and lifted his hips, begging for more.

RONI SMILED, A SIREN'S smile full of seduction, as she guided him to her center and then slowly, maddeningly slow, joined with him.

He held his breath, shocked by the feel of her. By the feel of rightness at being with her.

Her gaze locked with his, she moved. Barely. Entering leisurely into the rhythm of lovemaking. He guided her, his hands at her hips, urging her on.

"Eres tan linda," he said, because she was beautiful. Strong. Everything he could ever want, and he couldn't get enough of her as she rode him, drawing them ever higher. Moving together until her breath caught and she tumbled over, climaxing above him.

He caught her then, cradling her gently in his arms. Shifting to lie her on the soft cushions of the couch as he started to move again, seeking his own release. Wanting to bring her pleasure once again.

HER BODY WAS still alive with the aftermath of her climax when he started driving her upward again, and she wanted to experience his pleasure with him.

She wrapped her arms around him, urging him on. Kissing him, taking his breath into her, until her body responded to his and that moment came. That shattering moment binding them as they came together, breaths mingling.

Body shaking, Trey settled onto his side and tucked her against him on the narrow width of the sofa. His arms were around her and she buried her head against his chest to listen to the strong lub dub of his heart.

Neither of them said anything. What was there to say? she thought, even as the little voice in her head warned, *Are you kidding? You just made love—*

Had sex, she challenged. Granted, amazing mindblowing sex with the man of her dreams, but then came another realization.

With the man she was lying to, even if she hadn't really done anything to help IAD. But she had kept that from him even when she had asked him to trust her.

It was like an icy bucket of water being tossed on her.

She escaped his arms and grabbed up the dress and the torn remnants of her thong. *Dios mio*, she didn't even know when that had happened.

"Roni? What's wrong, Roni?" he said, easing up on his arm while he watched her hastily grabbing her clothing and shoes.

"We need to clean up. Anyone could walk in here at

any time," she said, clutching her things to her chest, feeling suddenly way too naked. Too exposed.

She didn't give him time to reply and rushed away.

TREY WAS LEFT to look at her retreating back as Roni raced into her bedroom. The door slammed shut like a loud clap of thunder.

He had wanted to tell her that not anyone could walk in at any time since access to the floor was locked down after 10:00 p.m. and before 7:00 a.m. for any keys other than the one for the penthouse.

Regardless, he didn't get what had just happened. How had it gone from that very nice, almost humbling feeling of being one after their amazing lovemaking to this?

He grabbed his clothes and shoes. Shook his head when he realized he hadn't taken off the ankle holster with his weapon. He took a step toward his room and the aches from the physical exertions of the night slowly started to register.

Aches in his ribs and shoulder. He'd hit the bumper of a car when he'd pulled Roni down to protect her.

Roni, he thought and glanced toward her closed door. He hoped he hadn't just ruined everything with her and chastised himself. He should have known better. They'd just survived a shooting and their emotions had been running high.

Too high? Had he taken advantage of her when she'd been way too vulnerable?

He didn't have time to think about that as his smartphone alerted him to a new email.

With a quick glance, he confirmed it was from Rogers, who had stayed behind to get the video from the hotel's CCTV system.

Time to get back to work.

SHE'D SHOWERED TO wash away the memory of him and the maelstrom of emotions after their lovemaking, but she didn't linger in the warm water, aware that they still had a lot to do that night.

When she exited her bedroom, Trey was at the dining room table, working on a laptop. He had showered as well, and his hair was still wet and slicked back from his face.

A stone-hard face that gave nothing away as to what he was feeling. But maybe that lack of emotion was telling in and of itself.

Maybe it hadn't meant as much to him as she'd thought.

She reined in her own emotions. She had to stay professional regardless of her earlier lack of control.

When he noticed her, he said, "I made some coffee. Thought we might need the boost."

She poured herself a cup, walked over and sat next to him. He used a remote to power up the television and bring up a video onto the screen. "Rogers sent this a short time ago."

He clicked a key and played the video of the car racing around the corner. He stopped it as the image of the car came into the center of the image, clearly displaying the muzzle fire from some kind of automatic weapon and a shadowy view of the driver. Even if it wasn't a clear view, it was obvious the driver was masked and gloved.

"I think the brass on the street was .223 Remington rounds."

Trey nodded and said, "I agree. That means he was likely using an AR-15."

The video advanced and Trey paused it when the back license plate bumper was visible.

"Do we have an owner yet?" Roni asked.

"We do, but the car had been reported stolen barely an hour earlier. The owner finished his shift and when he went to his car, it was gone. He'd parked it around Thirteenth and Collins," Trey advised and ran the rest of the video.

As she watched, different views popped onto the monitors from the multiple cameras on the hotel. She confirmed from those videos that the shooter had been masked and gloved. When Trey flashed a still image taken from one of the views, she examined it carefully.

"He looks like a tall man. Over six feet based on the height of his head," she said and walked to the monitor to point out the shooter's head position.

"Broad as well. Strong to be holding and firing the AR with one hand while driving with the other," Trey said.

"Like Ramirez. I'd say he's about 6'2" or so. Anderson is as tall but not as stocky. This guy's stocky, but it could just be the jacket," Roni said and once again motioned to what was visible of the shooter's body through the windshield.

"How did he know where we were? Your new partner?" Trey said. He shut off the monitor and got up to pace.

"Both Heath and the captain knew Wilson was on

Chapter Fifteen

oni's three days away from the station were almost
er, but there was no way she was going back when
r life was still in danger, and they still had to find the
issing college students.

But Trey's gut told him they were closer now that
ey'd pretty much eliminated Wilson as being respon-
le.

With Sophie and Rob's help, they had enough to
ve the payments into Doug's bank accounts were
tored. They had a possible link from MCP Enter-
es to the location on Terminal Island. Doug was the
to both as well as a link to Walsh. But to tie them
gether in order to be able to get warrants, Roni was
g to have to share that she'd seen his partner with
h. Unfortunately, if the press got hold of that, they
going to make his partner look dirty.

hated the thought of that, but there was no way
d it. He would make sure, however, that the real
got out once they were able to prove it.

came out of her bedroom in a sedate cream-
blouse and tailored black pants, looking very
ional and determined. That was obvious from

our radar. At least until we could get enough information on Walsh for another warrant," she said.

Trey was shaking his head as he paced. He whirled
on her. "Maybe someone who has both our phone numbers, right? Just like we found Eddie's phone, they found
us."

He grabbed his cell phone from his sweatpants
pocket and waggled his fingers for Roni to give him
hers. "We need to stop anyone from accessing these
phones."

She watched in surprise as he headed to the elevator,
and she raced after him. They went down to the main
offices where he turned and rushed toward a room a
few feet away. Light spilled from the room into the hall.

Following him, she realized they had reached Sophie
and Rob's tech center. Despite the late hour, they were
both still working on their computers.

Trey snapped his fingers, searching for a word as he
said, "What's the name of that bag thing—Fahrenheit?"

"You mean Faraday?" Rob said, while reaching for
what looked like a poly bag sitting on a shelf just in
front of his computer. He tossed it to Trey, who caught
it in one hand, dropped the phones in and sealed the bag.

Sophie pulled pods from her ears. "Someone tracked
you?"

"Possibly," he said and looked at his two cousins.
"You're not still here for us, are you?"

With a shrug, Rob said, "Not entirely. We had some
of our own work to catch up on."

"Nothing else so far on the bank accounts, but we're
still working on it," Sophie said.

"We appreciate that," Roni said.

Trey echoed her thanks. "We do appreciate it and maybe you should go get some rest."

"We will. In the meantime, there are some burner phones in that box over there. Prepaid cards as well," Rob said and gestured to a cardboard box holding more than a dozen cheap phones.

"Again, thanks," Trey said, grabbing two of them and then Roni's hand. With a tug, he led her back to the elevator and used the keycard to open access to the penthouse.

At her questioning look, he explained. "During certain hours, there's no access to the penthouse unless you have the right key."

The fact that their privacy had been guaranteed earlier did nothing to keep away the flood of heat that swept across her cheeks. Tilting her head up at a defiant angle, she said, "Might have been nice of you to let me know."

One dark brow shot upward. "Would it have changed anything?"

Deciding to be saucy to hide what she was really feeling, she said, "I might not have rushed."

As the elevator door opened, she snatched one of the phones from his hand while he stood there dumbfounded.

Good, she thought.

When the elevator door started to close, he rushed off and followed her to the center of the room. She waved the phone in the air and said, "When technology works it's great, but when it doesn't—"

"Like now when they used it against us," he said.

She nodded. "I know all we have about Walsh and

Santana is fairly circumstantial, but I think use it. Especially since we don't think Wils pect anymore."

"I've heard you can be persuasive with he said.

"I can, especially when we're talking abou ing women. Let's round it all up and see if w vince the DA to give us warrants for searches home and car."

He smiled, his earlier stone face replaced ish grin that always made her stomach do a li

"Let's get to work," he said.

the expression on her face as she walked over and grabbed the folder with the materials they had prepared last night in order to secure a search warrant for Walsh's home and office, and other records. After assembling what little they had on Santana, they'd opted to wait to ask for any warrants against him.

Hopefully they could get Walsh into an interview room and get him to make a mistake. Break him to find those women before they were either killed or sold off into slavery.

When she tucked the folder under her arm, she lifted her gaze to his and pride filled him. "I'm ready."

He nodded. "You are. Let's go."

They had called Rogers the night before and he had arranged for them to meet with an assistant district attorney to review their warrant application and request. Hopefully the ADA would find that what they had was enough to get a judge to issue the warrant.

They reached the courthouse in less than fifteen minutes and ADA Maria Morales was waiting for them in the lobby. The young woman immediately recognized them and ushered them through security and into a meeting room.

"We appreciate you meeting with us, Maria," Roni said as she laid out the search warrant application, affidavit with their reasons and evidence, and other materials on the surface of the table.

"I couldn't say no, Roni. You know how important it is for our office to get this under control," the ADA said as she sat to review the materials.

"I do, especially since Miami-Dade is one of the nation's worst areas for human trafficking," Roni said and sat with Maria to explain the various materials they had assembled in support of the search warrant.

Trey stood by, proud of what they had done together, but even more proud of how Roni was handling the meeting with the ADA. Together the two women made a few amendments to the application for the search warrant and then the ADA sat back and sucked in a deep breath.

The words burst from Maria's mouth. "I understand from your affidavit that you believe Walsh tried to run you down."

Roni's lips tightened into a hard line. "I believe it was him."

"What about last night's shooter?" the ADA pressed.

Roni shook her head. "We're not able to confirm Walsh was behind that."

Maria risked a look at Trey and then at Roni. "You've done a good job and I'll do my best to convince the judge," she said, as she gathered the papers together and stood.

But as she went to walk out, Roni said, "We need absolute confidentiality on this, Maria. The last leak from the DA's office cost us precious time."

Nodding, the ADA said, "I understand, and we're still trying to get to the bottom of that."

"We appreciate that, ADA Morales," Trey said, wanting to keep it amicable with the ADA.

With a dip of her head in acknowledgment, the ADA walked out of the meeting room.

Trey walked over and sat kitty-corner to Roni. "You did good."

"*Gracias*, but I couldn't have done it without you,"

she said and hesitated, as if she wanted to say more, but then her phone rang.

She shot a quick look at it and said, "It's the captain."

Turning on the speaker, she laid the phone on the table between the two of them.

"Good morning, Captain. I have Trey here with me," she said.

"Good morning. I have a team ready to execute the warrant at Walsh's home as soon as you give the word," he said.

"The ADA just went to speak to a judge. Hopefully we'll know soon. Once we do, Trey and I will head to MCP Enterprises to execute the warrant there."

"We'll wait for your word," the captain said and ended the call.

Roni splayed her fingers on the table, clearly anxious.

"It's going to be okay, Roni." He wanted to offer her physical comfort with a touch but wasn't sure she'd be receptive to it after last night.

She drummed her fingers on the table. "I feel like there are still so many loose ends. Dangerous unknowns. Ramirez. The status of the DA staff member who might have leaked the warrant."

"But we've made progress. Look at everything we just gave ADA Morales. And we eliminated Wilson as a suspect."

With a reluctant nod, she smoothed her fingers across the surface of the table. "You're right and I keep on telling myself we'll find the missing women soon."

"We will," Trey said and finally gave in and laid his hand over hers to still their nervous motion.

HIS TOUCH BROUGHT so many conflicting emotions. Comfort. Need. Hope. For them. For the missing women.

But as the clock on the wall above them ticked away the minutes, hope dimmed.

Nearly an hour had passed when ADA Morales finally returned to the room, a broad smile on her face. "Sorry for the delay but we had someone in front of us. And it wasn't easy, but we got it," she said and waved the warrant in the air.

"*Gracias*, Maria!" Roni shouted. She shot to her feet and almost ripped the paper from the attorney's hand.

"Good luck," Maria said and stepped out of the way to let Trey and Roni rush out the door.

"I'll call the captain," Trey said as he kept pace beside her.

She wasn't sure her feet were even hitting the marble tiles of the courthouse she was moving so fast, but as she noticed him wincing, she slowed her pace. They were in the police sedan they had picked up that morning and headed the short distance to the MCP Enterprises building within minutes, lights flashing. But as fast as they were going, it didn't seem fast enough.

Roni thumped her fingers on her thigh and tapped her feet against the car floor, adrenaline racing through her. In front of the MCP Enterprises building, they screeched to a halt and left the car in a no-parking area with the lights still going. Two marked cruisers were already there, and the officers exited their vehicles and came over to them for instructions.

"We're here to execute a search warrant. The suspect is inside, and we don't know whether he will run when presented with the warrant."

The four officers nodded and one of them said, "There are only two ways in and out. The main lobby and the freight area. We can secure those as well as the perimeter."

"Thank you," Trey said, and they hurried toward the building.

The presence of the cars and officers caused a stir as people looked their way and some even approached to see what was up, but Trey and she ignored the lookie-loos and pushed through the lobby to the security guard's desk. The guard from the day before didn't hesitate to open the gate when they flashed their badges.

Her body vibrated, almost trembling, as they reached the MCP Enterprises floor. Walsh saw them as soon as they stepped out of the elevator with their badges exposed. Instead of playing it cool, he bolted through a door at the far side of the floor into the office space.

"Police!" she shouted at the receptionist and the security guard who had started to approach them once Walsh dashed out of the lobby area.

They bolted across the floor to give chase and Roni used her police radio to alert the officers on the ground to apprehend Walsh. "Suspect is on the run. White male, approximately six feet. Short sandy hair. Wearing dark blue suit and white shirt," she called out into the radio.

Inside the office space, people popped up in their cubicles, curious at what was causing the slammed doors and shouting. But Walsh was nowhere to be found.

A young woman pointed toward one wall and said, "He went down the stairs."

"Thanks," Trey said, and they rushed to the stairway.

In the stairwell they could hear the slap-slap of footfalls on the metal and cement of the steps.

She leaned over the railing, caught a glimpse of Walsh rushing down the stairs and shouted, "Stop, police!"

She radioed her fellow officers. "He's heading down staircase A."

"On it," one officer replied.

She faced Trey, who shook his head and muttered a curse. "My leg can't handle twenty stories."

Nodding, she said, "I'll meet you on the ground."

He cursed again but didn't argue. "Stay safe."

"You, too," she said and flew down the stairs, grabbing the railing and using it to vault down multiple steps at a time as she chased Walsh.

His footfalls were erratic on the stairs ahead of her as Walsh likewise took multiple steps at a time. As she hit one landing, her ankle twisted, but she ignored the pain to keep on pushing toward her suspect.

At another landing, she realized she could no longer hear him in front of her and Trey was radioing his fellow officers, "Watch the elevators, staircases, and the freight elevator."

"Roger," the four other officers acknowledged.

She tried to enter the main building on her floor, but it was a no-access floor. Pushing down, she had to go another two levels before she could reenter. She raced across the floor to staircase B, thinking that Walsh must have re-entered at that point and confident that Trey and the other officers would handle the other access points.

A quick look and listen in staircase B was a negative, so she hurried to the elevator bank and pushed the call button, her mind racing with what might be happening with Walsh, who had clearly been ahead of her on the stairs and must have gone to an elevator.

"I've got eyes on him in the lobby. He's headed to the front of the building," one of the officers said.

"I'll intercept," another officer said.

Trey jumped on a second later. "I see him. Giving chase, but need assistance."

Roni cursed and was about to head for the stairwell again when the elevator doors opened. She jumped on and pushed the button for the lobby, her heart racing from her headlong flight down the stairs. Adrenaline speeding through her veins.

"Get down. Get down now," she heard across the radio as the elevator reached the main floor.

Running across the length of the lobby, she couldn't see either Trey or any of the officers and fear made her stomach lurch.

Through the glass of the oculus and the front doors she could see a crowd had gathered between the doors and the police cruisers.

Trey's voice came across the radio. "We got him. All officers meet in front."

She rushed out and had to force her way past the crowd, urging people aside. At the edge of the crowd, an officer was keeping them away from the area where another of the officers had Walsh on the ground while Trey cuffed him.

Her knees went weak at the sight of their suspect in custody and Trey and the other officer safe and sound. A second later, the two other officers met them.

Trey grabbed Walsh's arm and hauled him to his

feet. "Miguel Walsh," he said, but Walsh immediately started protesting.

"You've got no reason to arrest me," Walsh said, chin up defiantly as he tugged free from Trey's hold.

Roni slapped the warrant against his chest. "We have a search warrant."

She glanced at the officer who had been securing the lobby and then the crowd and said, "Did you identify yourself as an officer when you were in the lobby area?"

"I did, and the suspect ignored my command to stop," the officer stated.

She turned to Walsh. "You ignored instructions from Officer Rojas and me. We are therefore taking you into custody while we execute the search warrant."

With a jerk of her head, she instructed the officers to take him away and after they had bundled him into one of the cruisers, she breathed a sigh of relief.

Resting her hands on her hips, she glanced toward Trey and the two uniformed officers still standing there, waiting for instructions.

"Officer Rojas. Please assist Detective Gonzalez with the search of the suspect's vehicle. Officer Singh, you're with me."

Chapter Sixteen

The physical searches at Walsh's home, the MCP offices and his car yielded a cell phone, a briefcase filled with hundred-dollar bills and his passport.

Trey handed Roni the evidence bag with Walsh's cell phone. "With Sophie and Rob's assistance, the PD tech squad was able to hack the phone. Walsh wasn't using a burner. He had a burner phone app on his personal smartphone."

Roni shook her head in amazement. "That may make our lives easier."

Trey couldn't agree more. "We're already working to get the cell phone records on his personal device as well as those in the app. Hopefully there will be a pattern to point us in the direction of his associates."

He continued by spreading out about a dozen photos of Walsh with different women. "We also got these selfies from the phone."

"What an idiot," Roni said and leaned over the photos, examining them carefully. As her body did a little jump, he realized she'd seen it as well. She pointed to one photo. "This is one of the women from Terminal Island."

Trey nodded. "It is. We're running the other photos

through facial recognition software to try and identify them. Plus, the EXIF data will confirm when the photos were taken and possibly where, unless he turned off location data on the photo app."

Roni peered at the photos again and set aside one of them, obviously troubled by it. "There's something familiar about this one," she said and pointed to the woman's face.

"Is she one of your missing persons?" Trey wondered aloud and stood to also peer more intently at the photo.

With a bobble of her head, Roni said, "I don't think so. But I've seen that face before."

"Maybe we'll get a hit from the facial recognition," he said, but he could tell that Roni didn't want to wait that long.

"I know the assist from the tech will help us get the info faster than we used to, but we can only hold Walsh for 24 hours without charging him."

"Then let's get him in the box and talk to him. See how he responds to these photos. Ask him about that briefcase filled with money," Trey said.

Roni nodded and scooped up all the photos. "I agree."

Trey reached for the phone and called the officer responsible for the holding cells. "Please bring Miguel Walsh up to the interrogation room. Thanks."

They were walking out of the conference room when Captain Rogers approached and motioned them back into the space. He closed the door behind them and said, "I just got a call from the DA's office. One of their staff, Sylvia Reyes, didn't come in to work today and they can't track her down."

"Do they think she's the one who leaked the information on the tracking warrant?" Roni asked.

Rogers raked a hand across his short dark curls and blew out harsh breath. "They didn't get to interview her yesterday, but she knew they would be calling her in today."

"She ran," Trey said, but Roni immediately added, "Or someone silenced her."

Rogers nodded. "Either way, we'll do a welfare check. If that doesn't pan out, I'll get Sergeant Williams to track her phone to locate her. We're also pulling the call records from her phone at the DA's office. Info should be here within an hour. I'll get Williams working on that as well."

"We were just going to interview Walsh," Roni advised.

Rogers curtly dipped his head. "Keep me posted," he said and walked out of the conference room and back to his office.

Trey sneaked a look at Roni as he said, "He's not happy."

Sighing, she tucked her arms across her chest. "I get it. Someone gets to our witnesses again and again. Eddie and now this Sylvia."

She didn't mention the two attacks on her life, but Trey couldn't ignore them even if she wanted to downplay them. "And your safety."

She shook them off with a sharp wag of her head. "That's just part of the job."

"When I said almost the same thing you called me glib. Reminded me about how my family worries about my safety. Well, I worry about yours," he said and cupped her cheek.

RONI APPRECIATED HIS concern, but not at work where others could see and misinterpret it. Or worse, think that she was using Trey and his family to move her way up in the department.

"*Gracias*, but no PDA here," she said, and laid her hand over his, guiding it away.

Trey's look turned grim. "Let's go talk to Walsh."

She nodded in agreement. As they headed over to the interview room, her partner Williams walked over.

"I've got the techs tracking Reyes's phone and I'm waiting on the info. Mind if I watch the interrogation?" Heath asked and lifted his chin in the direction of the room with the one-way mirror and video recording equipment.

"I'd like that. We need a fresh eye at his reactions," Roni said and invited him into the room with a wave of her hand.

"Will do," Heath said.

After he closed the door to the viewing area, Trey and she entered the interrogation room.

Walsh slouched in a chair, arms tucked over his chest, straining the fabric of his dark blue suit. They'd removed his tie but had yet to put him in the orange jumpsuit they'd use if they charged him. He had a belligerent glare on his handsome face as they sat and identified themselves for purposes of the recording and asked him to do the same.

"My full name? Miguel Alejandro Walsh," he said, enunciating each syllable in challenge.

"Thank you, Mr. Walsh. Do you acknowledge that you were read your Miranda rights when we took you into custody?" she said.

"Yeah, you did, and yeah, I understand them. What I don't understand is why I'm here," he said and shot up from his slouch into a more active posture, resting his forearms on the edge of the table and using his hands to emphasize his question.

With a calm nod, Roni continued. "You work at MCP Enterprises as a security guard. Is that accurate?"

"It is and again, why am I here?"

"How long have you worked there?" she asked, keeping her voice neutral. She intended to let Trey get irritated, possibly even aggressive, in the hopes Walsh would make a slip.

As if sensing that they weren't going to answer any of his questions, he said, "Two years."

"What are your responsibilities there?"

With a shrug of broad shoulders, he said, "I guard the reception area."

"Anything else?" she asked, lifting a brow in emphasis.

He denied it with a careless shake of his head and said, "Nothing else."

Perfect, she thought. "We spoke to a number of the individuals employed at MCP. They told us that you also run errands for the CEO, Mr. Santana. Why would they say that?"

A little of his bravado fled. "Maybe I do that every now and then. Not often. It's not in my job description."

Roni waited the space of a breath, not wanting to give away that she knew he was lying because they'd seen him go into Santana's office. With every lie he was just going to dig a deeper hole for himself. "Can you tell us what *is* in your job description?"

He relaxed a little again and regained his earlier arrogant bravado. "I watch the reception area. Man the

lobby desk on the first floor if they need a break. Sometimes work the loading dock if there's something suspicious or if a money transfer is happening for the bank
in the building."

"What about these errands you run for Mr. Santana?"

Walsh stiffened in the seat, leaned back into that
slouch again and tucked his arms across his chest. "I
go down to the bank to get him cash. Pick up his dry
cleaning, Arturo Fuentes and Balvenie 21."

Trey let out a low whistle of appreciation at the mention of the pricey cigars and Scotch, and Roni offered
her own surprised chuckle. "He likes the finer things,"
she said and continued her questioning. "Sounds like
routine stuff," she said and made a pretense of scrib-
bling down notes on a pad in front of her.

"It is. Like I said, I don't know why you brought
me here," he said, throwing his hands up in the air in
disgust.

Roni looked at Trey in a way that said, "Tag, you're
it."

Trey dipped his head to confirm. "Miguel. Man to
man, here," he said and gestured with his finger between the two of them. "You're getting him money.
Clothing. Fancy cigars and Scotch. We both know something's missing in that picture."

Walsh blew out a laugh but his gaze narrowed in
anger. "I'm not a pimp, *mano*."

Trey held his hands up in a "who knows" gesture.
"How much do you make at MCP? $40K? $50K?"

"Six figures, *mano*. $100K," Walsh scoffed with a
laugh.

Trey shook his head ruefully and let out a low whistle. "Hear that, Lopez. Maybe you and me should quit the force and work for Santana."

"Maybe, Gonzalez. I guess that explains that fancy house in Coral Gables, except not even $100K will get you a house like that. Or a briefcase filled with cash," Roni said and pulled out pictures of the briefcase.

"Does it look like a go bag to you, Detective Lopez?" Trey said sarcastically.

"It does, Detective Gonzalez. Which makes me wonder why you'd need one," Roni said and stared hard at Walsh.

"You always have to be ready to go. You're *Cubanos*, *verdad*? You know," he said, gesticulating with his hands, trying to convince them.

"*Mano*, give us a break. The house. The money. The special little errands for Santana," Trey said. Opening the folder in front of him, he spread out the selfies.

"Women. Santana pays you to get women for him," he said while Walsh started waving his hands.

"I'm not saying another thing," Walsh said.

Trey separated one photo from the pack and jabbed a finger at the picture. "We found this woman in a storage container on Terminal Island. The property that container was sitting on is owned by MCP Enterprises," he lied, but hoping they could prove the connection in court.

Walsh's gesticulations got even more agitated, and he repeated again, "I'm not talking."

He wasn't talking but he also hadn't said the magic words, and until he asked for a lawyer, Trey intended to keep on pressing.

"Detective Lopez saw you with my partner the night he was murdered," Trey said, real anger creeping into his tone as he thought of how Doug had died that night. How he himself might have died.

Roni laid a hand on Trey's arm to rein him in and calmly said, "Do you know what the felony murder rule is, Miguel? If you had any connection to what happened to Detective Adams, you spend the rest of your life in prison. Or if you're lucky, forty years."

Trey slapped the table, the sound as loud as a gunshot. He pushed to his feet and leaned toward Walsh. "But you also tried to run down Detective Lopez. That's another thirty years, *mano*. Either way, you'll rot in jail."

"I'm not talking. I want a lawyer," Walsh shouted and shot up out of his chair. He started pacing back and forth in the room, muttering, "I want a lawyer."

Trey shared a look with Roni who said, "Let the record show that Mr. Walsh requested counsel."

Roni rose, turned and motioned to her partner through the one-way mirror.

He came in seconds later with a uniformed officer, who walked over to Walsh.

At Roni's nod, the uniform cuffed Walsh as Roni said, "Mr. Walsh, we're arresting you for evading a peace officer and resisting arrest."

"I didn't do anything, I'm telling you. I had nothing to do with anything," he said and jerked away from the uniformed officer who was trying to lead him from the interrogation room.

Trey raised his hand to stop the officer. "You asked for counsel, Miguel. Have you changed your mind? Are you willing to talk to us without counsel?"

Walsh jerked upright and quieted, as if considering it, but then he said, "No. I didn't do anything. I want to call a lawyer."

Chapter Seventeen

Walsh would be getting his call, but they weren't going to rush into another interrogation with him and a lawyer without having something to place more pressure on him. They needed to break him.

Her three days of "vacation" were over and with confidence that her new partner wasn't part of the problem, Roni sat with Trey and Heath in the conference room and set up the white board to review all the evidence they had gathered so far.

She tacked up photos of her missing women as well as Walsh, Trey's dead CI Eddie and their fellow officer Doug Adams. For good measure, she also wrote the name of the DA's missing employee, Sylvia Reyes.

Trey and Heath began to read off the info they had on each of them so far and Roni wrote it on the white board. As they got to the phone records for Walsh and Reyes, they spread the printouts on the table, began reviewing them and immediately noticed that there was one number that both Walsh and Reyes had recently phoned.

"Too much coincidence," Roni said as she wrote the number down on the board.

"I doubt it's still active, but we should try," Trey said and dialed the number from his burner phone. A rough jerk of his head gave her the answer a second before he said, "No longer active. But we should still ask for the call detail records. They may give us more info."

Lips tight, she glanced at Doug's photo. She hated to do it but had no choice. Gesturing to Doug's photo, she said "Do we have anything in the phone records that connects Walsh with Doug or with Reyes?"

Trey hauled out another printout. Heath and he started to look through the lines of data, but after a few minutes, Trey straightened away from the papers. "I see the same number here and here," he said, pointing to the data from Walsh's burner phone app and Reyes's phone at the DA's office.

"That's progress," Roni said.

"It is, but there are so many other numbers. Do we have these digitally?" he asked Heath.

Her partner nodded. "We have digital files for all of them."

"Great. Let's email those to Sophie and Rob to search for more similarities in the three files," Roni said. Better to have the computers deal with things like that than waste their time.

A knock at the door drew their attention and Captain Rogers marched in, a grim look in his eyes. "The DA had local PD do a welfare check at Ms. Reyes's home. No one answered. They spoke to neighbors who said they had not seen her since she left for work the day before. One of them had a key in case of emergencies and gave PD access to the home. Yesterday's mail was still on the floor by the mail slot. It also didn't appear that anyone had slept in the bed."

"Walsh and Reyes both made calls to the same burner phone in the last two days. That's too much co-incidence, Captain," Roni said.

Rogers nodded emphatically. "You're right. We have to assume something's happened to Ms. Reyes. We'll issue a BOLO for her and also for her vehicle. I'll keep you posted if we get any kind of hit," he said and ex-ited the room.

Roni added the information about Reyes's disappear-ance to the white board, stepped back and looked at it. "I'm not sure it's Santana that connects them. I think it's possibly our dirty cop."

"And we're no closer to finding him," Heath said with an exasperated sigh.

Roni watched as Trey bit back a response. He'd said he hadn't liked Williams when Doug and he had worked with him. He still seemed unhappy, but they had too much to put together and needed her partner's assis-tance.

"We're not, but we'll get there," she said, trying to stay positive. Gesturing to all the paperwork they'd gathered, she said, "We have the dates the young women disappeared. The approximate times. Let's go back to those phone records and see what kind of activity we have on Walsh's phones."

She walked over to stand between the two men, pro-viding a buffer, as the three of them perused the phone records for specific nights. As she had expected, there was a great deal more activity, especially in the later hours. She ran a finger across those calls. "Probably to another burner phone, like he was signaling someone. Maybe to make an exchange. Once the exchange happened, the calls stopped."

Trey motioned to the list. "That first column is the switch that the call is hitting, probably when it comes off the cell towers and has to be routed to the next location," he explained.

Heath jumped in with, "But these two columns are the cell sites that picked up the calls."

"Even though Walsh shut off location services on his phone, these records should be able to give us a general location. Same with the burner phones," Roni said.

Trey looked at Heath and Roni braced herself as he said, "I'll call the provider to get the location of the cell sites. Do you mind working with the ADA for a warrant for the call detail records for those burner phones?"

Heath pointed a finger at Trey in a friendly "got it" gesture. "Will do. I'll be back as soon as we have those records."

TREY HADN'T MISSED the way Roni tensed beside him or that she'd used herself as a buffer between him and Heath. "Maybe he's not as bad as I thought," he said with a wave of his hands.

"Maybe. In the meantime, let's get this cell site info. I'll plot the locations for MCP, Walsh's home and all the other places on a map," Roni said.

"Hopefully it'll help us narrow where we have to search," Trey said and the two of them went to work.

He tracked down someone at the phone provider who was able to identify which cell sites were used. As the representative started rattling off longitudes and latitudes, Trey said, "Would you mind emailing that information to me for our records? Also, what's the range on that cell site?"

"These cell sites are in a busy area so there are a lot of them. The caller will be relatively close to the tower," the representative said.

"How close is close?" Trey pressed.

"It could be as little as the length of a football field or at most half a mile or so," the phone rep said.

"Thanks. That's a big help," he said. With that small a distance to place where the calls were being made and received, it might help them identify the area where the transfer of the women had been made.

When he received the email on his phone, he sent the information to the printer located in the squad room and went to retrieve the report. As he exited the conference room, he noticed Ramirez and Anderson walking to Captain Rogers's office. Rogers had his door closed and was on the phone.

The two IAD detectives noticed Trey as well and detoured in his direction.

"Gonzalez. Didn't expect to see you here," Ramirez said and lifted his chin to peer down his nose at Trey.

"Thought you were on medical leave," his sidekick Anderson added, placing his hands on his hips and pulling his shoulders back in a challenging gesture.

"I was going stir-crazy, so Captain Rogers let me come back on desk duty," he said, which while not totally true wasn't a lie either. Rogers was on board with Trey to find the missing women and the truth about his dead partner.

Shifting the focus to keep them from asking more

questions about the investigation, he said, "Do you have anything about Doug or his killers yet?"

Anderson was better off not playing poker since his normally pink complexion turned an even brighter pink and he shot an almost pleading look at his partner.

Ramirez ignored Anderson and said, "You should know better than to ask, Gonzalez. Everything we do in IAD is confidential."

Trey held his hands up in a surrender gesture.

Ramirez jerked his chin in the direction of the conference room. "Lopez in there?"

"We're working on something right now. I recommend calling her to schedule a meeting," he said and didn't wait for Ramirez to respond.

He hurried to pick up the printed email to add to their file and so Roni could pin the locations to the map she was preparing. As he walked away, it felt like Ramirez's gaze was stabbing knives in his back. When he snagged the paper from the printer, Ramirez and Anderson were still waiting by the entrance to Rogers's office.

Impatience radiated in every line of Ramirez's body. He had jammed his hands into his pants pockets, and he was jiggling the change there while rocking back and forth on his heels.

Rogers's office was just feet away from the conference room. He half expected Ramirez to push in to see what they were working on, but a moment later Rogers set down the phone receiver, stood up and opened the door to his office.

Ramirez shot Trey another angry glare; Anderson a sheepish one.

Trey ignored them and returned to the conference

room. For safety's sake, he locked the door, not wanting a surprise visit from Ramirez with so much information up on their white board.

"Ramirez and Anderson are here to see Rogers," he said as he walked over to where Roni was working on the laptop.

She peered at the closed door and then up at him. "I wonder what they have for Rogers."

"Ramirez hauled out the "confidential" card when I asked," Trey said and placed the email on the table. "Do you think you can plot the cell site locations on the map?"

Roni leaned over to look at them and nodded. "I may not be your tech guru cousins, but I'm not a Luddite."

"I guess I am because I couldn't do it," he confessed, not above admitting his limitations.

"Showing your age," she teased and flashed him a saucy smile.

He playfully tugged on a lock of her hair. "Four years isn't all that much, but if it is, mind your elders," he kidded.

Roni chuckled and leaned closer to the email to read the data, narrowing her eyes to stare at the small print. "Could you please read it aloud while I enter it?"

"I guess I'm not the only one getting old," he mocked, but did as she asked, reading off the longitude and latitude coordinates that the phone provider rep had given him for the cell sites.

Once she had entered them all, she said, "What's the range?"

"Rep said the maximum range was about half a

mile," he said and with a few keystrokes, she'd drawn circles to reflect that on her map.

"This is really helpful," she said and displayed the map on the big monitor at one end of the room.

"It is," Trey said as he looked at the overlap between the places from their investigations that Roni had already located on the map and the areas where Walsh had either sent or received phone calls.

"This confirms he was in the area of the clubs when the women went missing. It also confirms he may have been at the club when I saw him with Doug," Roni said and grabbed a laser pointer to highlight the circle defining the max range of the cell site.

"If we don't push it to the max," she began and hit a few keys, presumably to tighten the range since the circles on the maps shrunk. One pin stuck out like a sore thumb.

"The club where it all began the night Doug was killed is in this area," Trey said and walked up to the monitor. "And this is the area on Terminal Island."

He gestured to a pin that Roni had entered for another cell site. "This is a totally new area. Indian Creek if I had to guess," he said, circling all around the location with his finger.

"It is Indian Creek, but the home address we have for Santana is on Fisher Island. But the calls were made in this area when the women were taken. Let's see what we have here," Roni said and barely a minute later a satellite view of the map displayed. With another few keystrokes, she moved the focus of the map and magnified it to reveal the buildings and streets in the area.

"It's mostly private homes. Expensive private homes,

which would jive with the one witness who says she went to a party at an upscale home," Trey said but shook his head. "Who would risk that at their own home?"

RONI PONDERED IT carefully because Trey was right about the risk of using a personal home in a criminal enterprise like they had uncovered. "If we use RICO we seize the house, and if it's a family home... You'd have to be pretty coldhearted if you've got a wife and kids like Santana does."

"Unless you're desperate for cash like he is," Trey reminded.

"Let's imagine that he is pretty desperate and needs to raise cash...in a legal way. What would he do?"

Trey tossed a hand up in the air and went with it. "He'd reach out to banks for loans or other businesspeople for investments."

Roni held up a finger. "If he goes the businesspeople route, he doesn't want them to know just how cashstrapped he is. He wants to wine and dine them while he tries to convince them to invest."

Trey nodded. "I'm with you so far. But why not have the party at his home or one of the nicer hotels or country clubs in the area?"

"Maybe because he's offering his guests things that aren't necessarily all that legal. And if he's involved with the trafficking, he wants somewhere the women can be held without being seen," Roni said. She leaned back in her chair and laid her hands on the edge of the table, drumming her fingers while she thought about it.

"Do you think it's possible that they're still in Indian Creek? It's over a week now," he said, concern ringing in his tone.

She blew out a frustrated sigh. "I'm not optimistic about that. But I do know how I would rent one of these homes if I wanted to," she said and used the laptop to bring up listings for an assortment of homes that were available for short-term and vacation rentals.

There were no rentals on Indian Creek Island, but when she expanded the range of the cell site, there were three different rentals along the waterfront in Bay Harbor Islands. Two of the properties were large Mediterranean-style villas with waterfront property and she pulled up the listings and scrolled through the photos. Both locations had boat docks.

"Easy enough to take the women to the dock and move them by boat to Terminal Island. Fewer prying eyes," Trey said.

"I agree," she said and switched over to a listing for a penthouse suite in a new boutique building. "This building has a strict 'no party' policy and it would be much harder to move anyone without being spotted."

"Looks like we have our marching orders," Trey said.

Chapter Eighteen

"We appreciate you helping us, Mimi," Roni said to the young woman who had managed to escape from one of the parties after being roofied. She was being kept in a safe house until they identified who had attempted to kidnap her.

Mimi laced her fingers together tightly and bounced her hands on the surface of the table. "I don't think I'll feel safe until this is all over."

"I understand," Roni replied and reassured Mimi with a gentle squeeze of her arm. "We're recording this interview, if that's okay with you."

Mimi nodded. "If it will help, I'm fine with that."

"Good. For the record, this is Detective Veronica Lopez interviewing Mimi Martell."

Roni pulled out pictures of the two locations they had downloaded from the rental site as well as some from other unrelated homes. She had mixed them up to not influence Mimi in any way, but the backs were labeled to identify them.

"Do any of these locations look familiar?"

Mimi leaned forward to peruse the photos. Ran her hands across them and picked one up, then put it down.

She did that several times, but finally pointed to three different pictures.

"I remember the house being beautiful, but like someone was trying too hard to make it look like an Italian villa." She snapped her fingers, jabbed at one photo and said, "I remember I bumped into a statue and skinned my thigh on it."

"Let the record show that Ms. Martell identified exhibits 10, 14 and 18," Roni said and set those pictures aside.

A knock came at the door and she called out, "Come in."

Trey walked in and did a quick bob of his head to indicate the lineup had been prepared.

Roni reached out to the witness again and said, "The lineup is ready if you are."

Mimi clenched her hands together but nodded. "I'm ready."

"Detective Lopez ending the interview with Ms. Martell," she said to stop the recording.

Mimi got to her feet shakily, wobbling so badly at one point that she had to brace a hand on the table to stay upright.

"Are you sure you're up to this?" Trey asked and reached out a hand to steady their witness.

Mimi slipped her hand into Trey's and nodded. "I'm ready."

Gripping Trey's hand tightly, she walked down the hall and into the area where they did the lineups. When Mimi entered, Trey guided her into the center of the room and released her hand, not wanting to open the door to a defense attorney to say he influenced her with his touch.

"Whenever you're ready," Roni said as she and Trey stood off to one side, ready to signal an officer to bring in Walsh and the other men they'd assembled for the lineup.

Mimi tipped her head up and down. "I'm ready."

Trey stepped out to inform the officer and as he returned, barely seconds later, the officer guided in six men of like height, hair color and build.

They'd done a good job with the lineup. Maybe too good, Roni thought, worried whether Mimi would be able to pick out Walsh. After all, Roni had had her doubts after seeing Miles Wilson, but then again, she'd only had a quick glance of Walsh with Doug and at the wheel of the car. But even those quick glances had been enough to have someone trying to kill her. If Mimi identified Walsh, they'd have to increase the security measures they had in place.

"Take your time," Trey said, his tone firm, but calming.

Mimi nodded, a little steadier this time. "Can I see the right side of their faces?" she asked.

Roni hit an intercom button and said, "Please face left."

The men in the lineup did as instructed, shifting to show their right profile.

Roni peered toward Mimi, who gestured to her own face, right by her ear, and said, "He has a small mole here."

"Okay. Can you identify who that is?" Trey asked, his tones patient, but level.

Mimi nodded and pointed toward the man holding up a placard with the number five. "That's him. He has the mole and I remember his features. He was the one at the club who took me to the party."

"Are you sure, Mimi?" Roni asked, wanting to be certain because Mimi had identified Walsh. With that they could hopefully, at a minimum, prosecute him for the use of the roofie and attempted kidnapping.

Mimi pulled her shoulders back and straightened, gathering her core of strength. "Yes. Without a doubt."

"Thank you, Mimi. Our officers will take you back to the safe house now," Trey said and gestured for her to leave the room, while Roni used the intercom to indicate that the lineup was over.

Outside the room, Roni again thanked Mimi and Trey led her to an officer who would take her back to the apartment where she was being protected. Roni returned to the interview room and gathered the photos to be added to the evidence they had already collected against Walsh.

When Trey returned to the conference room, he said, "I think that's enough to arrest Walsh for the roofie and kidnapping and to ask ADA Morales to file charges."

"And to ask for a search warrant at that house in Bay Harbor Islands. If Mimi did get scraped by that statue, there may be some of her DNA left on there to confirm that was the location. We may even get lucky and find other evidence," she said and dialed the ADA.

"Good afternoon, Maria. We think we've got him,

but we'll need another search warrant. We'll prepare the paperwork for the warrant and send it to you shortly."

"I'm in court until late afternoon but I can have another attorney review the warrant request as soon as you send it," the ADA said.

"Great. We appreciate the help," Roni said.

A knock came at the door and at her "Come in," her partner Heath entered.

He jerked his head in the direction of the squad room. "Walsh's attorney is here. They're waiting in an interrogation room."

"Good. I think it's time to show him some of our cards and see how he reacts. See if we can get him to finger someone else in exchange for a plea bargain," Roni said and looked over at Trey.

"I agree but I think we need to find out more about that house and who might have rented it. I can work on it if you want Heath to sit in on the interview with you," he said and jerked his head in the direction of the other man.

Roni was surprised again but understood what Trey was trying to do. "Heath, is that okay with you?"

Her partner shrugged and gestured toward the papers on the conference room table. "You two have been working together so far. I can do the digging on the house and let you know when the search warrant comes in. Plus, I think I may have a lead on one of the women in the photos."

"What kind of lead?" Roni asked.

"I thought I recognized her and started searching through some homicide reports. I think she's a Jane Doe who was found about a week before those college students were taken. Probably around the same time the sex workers were taken. I'm waiting for the file from Homicide," Heath advised.

Roni nodded. "Good work."

TREY MOTIONED TO their evidence. "Do you want to select what we're going to show Walsh?"

Roni nodded. "Sure." She walked over and started going through the papers, selecting only a few items, mostly pictures of the women and two from the house they'd identified as being the possible location for the abductions.

Trey examined the items and said, "Looks good. Are you ready to do the interrogation?"

"Yes," she said, but then added, "I'd like you to take the lead. Be the good cop to start."

He had no doubt she could handle the bad cop part. Her anger and worry about the missing women were a fire in her belly that wouldn't be extinguished until the women were found.

"Let's go," he said, snatching up the items she'd selected, and they headed to the interrogation room.

Once they'd introduced themselves and started recording, Walsh's attorney immediately jumped to his client's defense.

"I understand you interviewed my client without the presence of counsel. You understand anything he said will not be admissible."

If the man's dress and jewelry were any indication, he was an expensive lawyer. The suit was custom-made and beneath it was an expensive shirt—Egyptian cotton—and a silk tie. He wore a gold Rolex on one wrist, a thick gold bracelet on the other and a pinkie ring in a Cuban link pattern studded with diamonds. The longer strands of his fade were ruthlessly gelled into place.

"Mr. Jimenez, is it?" Trey asked and scrutinized the business card the lawyer had presented and passed it over to Roni. Like the clothing, the card radiated success from the weight of the card stock to the engraving and foil. It made him wonder who was footing the bill for Walsh's defense.

At the man's nod, Trey continued. "Your client was given and acknowledged his Miranda rights. As soon as your client requested an attorney, the interview was concluded. But now that you're here, we'd like to continue with the interrogation."

"My client has nothing else to say at this time," the attorney said. He clasped his hands and rested them on the table, totally confident in his abilities.

Even if Roni intended to play bad cop, Trey couldn't resist the urge to take this hotshot attorney down a few pegs.

"You should be aware that we have a witness who has identified your client as the man who drugged her, participated in her sexual assault and attempted kidnapping," Trey said.

"I already told you—" Walsh began, but his attorney stopped him with an outstretched arm.

"My client has nothing else to say," the attorney repeated.

"That's fine because we have plenty to say," Trey said and removed the selfies of Walsh posing with the woman from Terminal Island as well as the unidentified woman Heath thought might have been murdered.

He spread them across the table in front of Walsh and his counsel. Tapping at each of the women, he said, "This is your client, Mr. Jimenez. These photos came from his smartphone—"

"And we'll object to that search warrant on the basis you lacked probable cause," the attorney said smugly.

"And lose," Roni interjected and continued in a deadly calm voice. "We have more than enough evidence to support probable cause."

Before the lawyer could object again to anything else, Trey laid out the photos from the rental property Mimi had identified. It was impossible to miss the look of shock that skipped across Walsh's features.

"I guess the home looks familiar to your client based on his reaction," Trey said and locked his gaze with Walsh's. "You've been there and I'm sure our CSI team is going to find your prints and DNA all over that location."

"We'll object to that as well and win, Detective," the attorney said self-assuredly, but not before Trey detected a slight wobble in his earlier confidence.

Before he could say anything else, Roni jerked a thumb in the attorney's direction. "Someone's obviously paying him well to play all these lawyer games and I'm betting it's not you, Miguel. But you see these women?" she said harshly and angrily jabbed a finger at the photos. "These women know what you are. We believe this woman was murdered as part of your human trafficking ring. That makes three murders you'll be charged with in addition to all the other crimes."

Walsh nervously glanced at his attorney, his face pale. Despite the air conditioning in the room, beads of moisture dotted his upper lip and a line of sweat trailed down the side of his face.

"Tell us where the two college students are being held. If you help us, we can help you," Trey said, his tone almost cajoling.

"I… How can you help?" Walsh said, but his lawyer held his hand up to stop him.

"My client has nothing else to say," the attorney repeated, but his hand wavered.

"Is Santana paying your attorney to keep you quiet? Is he paying you to not implicate him? Money isn't going to do you much good when you're in prison for life," Roni said, her voice rising with each word.

The attorney slammed his hands on the table and abruptly stood up. "I'm ending this interview now. If you think you have enough—"

Roni shot to her feet and said, "Miguel Walsh. We're arresting you for the sexual assault and kidnapping of Mimi Martell, Aida Smith and Kristie Zachary, and the murders of Eduardo Angel and Detective Douglas Adams."

She reached into her waistband, took out her handcuffs and walked over to Walsh, who appeared shell-shocked as she urged him to his feet and cuffed him.

"Don't worry, Miguel. We'll have you out on bail in no time," the attorney said.

"I wouldn't count on that," Roni said as Trey opened the door to allow one of their uniformed officers to enter and take Walsh back to a holding cell and then jail.

As Walsh was being led out, he shot a frantic look over his shoulder at his counsel. "Do something, Jimenez. Get me out of here," he shouted as the officer led him away.

"Don't worry, Miguel," the attorney repeated, but he was obviously rattled by the charges Roni had just read off as she'd arrested Walsh.

"He should be worried, Mr. Jimenez. He's going to be spending a very long time in prison," Roni said, as she smiled and tucked her arms against her chest in a very confident pose.

Flustered, Jimenez grabbed his briefcase. "You'll be hearing from me."

He hurried out of the room, leaving Trey and Roni in the interrogation room. "That went well," Trey said, and Roni dipped her head in agreement.

"Walsh is scared. He knows we have him dead to rights. We'll just have to see how long he'll protect Santana and whoever is the dirty cop."

A dirty cop who was likely the one responsible for the drive-by shooting at the Del Sol, Trey thought.

"It's time to bring the other women in for another lineup," Trey said as they strolled toward the conference room.

"If they haven't already run out of town and gone somewhere else to earn their living," Roni said, sadness in her tone. The two sex workers had refused protection and likely fled the area out of fear of being killed.

Trey shook his head, disappointed by that possibility. "And maybe get hurt or killed by another john."

"Maybe. I'm hoping that what happened will make them think about changing their lives," she said as they entered the conference room and her phone chirped to warn she had a message. After a quick look at her phone, she said, "We got the warrant. Heath's ready to go to the location and wants to know if we want to go with him."

"Heck, yeah. I want to speak to the owner of that home and try to find out more about who rented it for those parties," Trey said.

"I agree. I'm hoping all the threads lead back to Santana—"

"And to Ramirez. My gut tells me he's the dirty cop," Trey said and tucked the photos back into their case file, but as he did so, he didn't fail to miss the slight wince Roni gave at the mention of the other man's name.

"You don't think—"

"There's something I have to tell you."

Chapter Nineteen

There was never going to be a good time for her confession, so now was as good a time as any.

She wrapped her arms around herself and blurted out, "Ramirez asked me to work with IAD to find out what happened with Doug."

Trey reared back as if slapped and his gaze nailed hers in accusation. "You said *no*, right?"

"I didn't," she said and at his shocked look, she held her hands out in pleading. "I wanted to clear Doug's name, but more importantly, I wanted to make sure IAD didn't go after you."

"Me?" he almost shouted and jabbed a finger in his chest. "You thought I might have something to do with Doug's murder?"

She walked over and laid a hand over his chest, but he flinched and stepped back. Shaking her head, she raked her fingers through her hair and blew out a frustrated breath. "No, of course not. But you know Ramirez can't stand you. He thinks your family's legacy with the force has opened doors for you and he resents that."

A sharp rap on the door caused them both to shout in unison, "What?"

Heath stood at the door, his brow furrowed, as he looked in at them. He held up a piece of paper. "Search warrant."

Roni nodded. "Got it. Time to go to Bay Harbor Islands."

She turned and walked away from Trey, but there was no avoiding the heat of his anger that chased her from the room.

Heath fell into place beside her while Trey followed as they left the station house and went to a sedan in the parking lot.

A heavy silence sat over them in the car as Heath drove to the address for the rental home in Bay Harbor Islands.

As her partner drove, Roni sat in the passenger seat, recalling all that their witness had told them about the party location she remembered and what had happened the night she was taken.

She couldn't imagine that whoever was doing this would only take one woman at a time. They had to make the most of their investment in renting the property.

But had they taken more than two women each time? Would that explain the other women in Walsh's selfies and the Jane Doe homicide that Heath thought was connected to their case?

Those questions and more stormed through her brain along with Trey's accusing stare as she'd told him about agreeing to help IAD. Not that she had. Too many things had happened too quickly, so it had been impossible to do so.

But would I have really done it if there had been time? she wondered.

The answer came immediately: *Yes*. If it would clear Doug's name and keep Trey safe, she definitely would have helped IAD.

Lost in her thoughts, it took the gentle stop of the car to pull her back to reality.

A CSI truck sat in front of the home, a beautiful Mediterranean-style villa just as described on the rental website and in the photos. The multimillion-dollar home was beautifully landscaped with assorted tropical foliage. The deep green of large elephant ear plants mingled with caladiums with bright pink, orange and white leaves. Low-lying bromeliads added their deep greens and reds along the borders. Tall birds-of-paradise added higher bursts of orange and red against the stucco walls of the home and the umbrella-like fronds of sago palms.

Towering royal palms shuddered as a strong breeze swept off the water behind the home interrupted the green expanse of the manicured lawn.

As the CSI members stepped from their truck, Heath, Trey, and she exited the sedan and walked up to the front door, which opened even before they reached it.

A young man stood at the door, wearing a University of Miami T-shirt and loose fleece shorts with the Miami orange and green.

Roni put the young man in his early twenties. He had a lean muscular build, sandy hair cut in a fashionable fade and scruffy stubble on a sharp jaw.

"Can I help you?" he said, puzzlement in his voice and narrowed gaze as it skipped from their badges to the CSI team.

Heath handed the search warrant to the young man. "We have a warrant to search the premises."

"I—I don't understand," he muttered, but didn't move to allow them to enter.

Roni jumped in to explain. "We have reason to believe this is a crime scene. Maybe we can go inside so we can discuss this?"

The young man hesitated but stepped aside and motioned for them to enter. Once inside, he finally looked at the warrant while the CSI agents fanned out to start working.

Roni gestured to Heath and Trey. "Sergeant Williams and Detective Gonzalez. I'm Detective Lopez. Are you the homeowner?"

He shook his head. "No, my parents own it. They're going to kill me."

"And you're…" she said, encouraging him to give his name.

"Oh, sorry," he said and held his hand out to shake theirs. "Ricky Martin, and yes, I get grief for that," he said with a friendly, but forced, smile.

"Ricky. We appreciate your cooperation. As I said earlier, your parents' home may be a crime scene. This property is listed for rental. Are you responsible for that?"

A grimace flitted across his features, and he rubbed the back of his neck, obviously worried. "My parents don't like Miami summers. They have a second home in the Berkshires and stay there for a few months."

"You decided to take advantage of their absence to rent out the home using Airbnb. How much do renters pay you for the use of the house?" Trey asked.

With a shrug, Ricky said, "I normally rent it for $1,800 a night, but I was worried about anyone having parties here. They can get out of hand."

"What did they pay you to rent your home for their parties?" Roni pressed.

He rubbed the back of his neck again and his gaze flitted across them and then to where the CSI agents were on the back patio, searching for evidence on the statues along the edge of the pool.

"Ricky?" she said again at his prolonged silence.

"He said it was for a business party," Ricky almost whined, as if finally sensing that this was really something to worry about.

"Who said?" Trey pushed.

"The guy renting this place. $5,000 cash each night with a guarantee that he would have the place spotless by the time they left," he finally admitted.

"Was this the guy?" Heath held up their sketch of Walsh, not wanting to show him a real photo to avoid tainting any later identification in a lineup.

Ricky leaned forward to examine the sketch and did a shaky nod. "I think so."

"Would you be willing to come to the station and identify him in a lineup?" Trey asked.

Ricky immediately nodded and said, "I will, but... I'm not in trouble, am I?"

Roni shared a look with Heath and Trey before returning her attention to Ricky. "You may want to reconsider who you rent to."

"I—I will. Seriously, I had no idea they were doing anything illegal. They said it was for parties to get investors for their company," he reiterated.

"Did they mention the name of the company?" Roni asked and at that, Ricky snapped his fingers.

"He gave me a card. Let me go get it," he said and

dashed off and up the stairs. He came bounding down minutes later, hand outstretched with a business card.

Heath snapped on a nitrile glove and took the card. Held it up so that Trey and she could see that it had an alias.

"Maybe we can get a fingerprint or touch DNA," Roni said as Heath slipped it into an evidence bag.

"Would you mind giving us a sample of your DNA and your fingerprints," Trey asked, and Ricky immediately acquiesced.

"I didn't mean to do anything, seriously. I just needed some extra cash while I go to school."

Roni suspected that the extra cash wasn't for tuition since anyone with a house this size could easily afford U of M. The money was more likely for vacations and other things, legal things she hoped.

"Can you provide us the dates when this individual rented the home?" Roni asked.

Ricky vigorously nodded. "I can," he said, and whipped out his phone. After swiping around, he rattled off a number of dates that her partner wrote down on a notepad.

"Thank you for that. We're going to look around while our CSI team finishes their investigation," Roni said.

Ricky held his hands wide in invitation. "Whatever you need," he said, clearly hoping he would avoid trouble by cooperating.

"Great," Roni said and turned to face Heath and Trey. "Let's split up and look around for anything out of the ordinary while the CSI guys do their thing. I'll take the upstairs."

Trey jerked his head in the direction of the pool area. "I'll look around outside."

"I'll do this lower level," Heath said.

They split up.

The upstairs level had five bedrooms and six bathrooms. Each bedroom had an en suite bathroom and walk-in closet. The furniture was all modern, minimalist and seemingly pristine, except for what she assumed was Ricky's bedroom.

It was what you might expect for a twentysomething college student. Notebooks, pens, highlighters, books, and dirty plates from an assortment of meals were scattered on a large desk.

A tangle of sheets and comforters covered a large king-size bed.

There was a smell in the room besides that of the half-eaten pizza on the desk: weed. The skunky smell was evident, confirming her earlier worries about where the rental monies were going.

She moved from bedroom to bedroom, checking in and around each space carefully. There wasn't a bit of dust anywhere or fingerprints on the surfaces of the furniture or in the bathrooms. She suspected that the homeowners regularly had housekeepers or cleaners who came in and Walsh's crew had probably done as promised after the parties.

That gave her little hope that they would find any fingerprints or other evidence, except possibly some DNA from one of the statues to prove Mimi Martell had been here the night she had escaped the human trafficking ring. But she was worried that after over two weeks, rain and sun had either washed away or deteriorated any DNA.

Despite that, Ricky's testimony would help, especially if he picked out Walsh in a lineup.

Since Walsh supposedly orchestrated the parties for a "business," maybe it was time to sweat Santana to gauge his involvement.

With one last sweep around the upstairs, she returned to the main floor where Heath was chatting with Ricky. Trey was outside with the CSI people, talking to them, but as if he had some sixth sense, he turned to look at her as she walked over to Ricky and her partner.

As Heath also gave her his attention, she shook her head "no."

Heath nodded and said to Ricky, "We'll need you to come down for a lineup and as I mentioned before, provide your DNA and fingerprints so we can eliminate you from any evidence we might obtain. If you have cleaning or housekeeping staff—"

"We do. My parents have someone come in once a week," Ricky immediately offered.

Heath nodded. "We need them to provide their DNA and fingerprints as well."

Ricky went white and said, "Is that really necessary?" He was obviously worried that whatever was happening during his unauthorized rentals would be revealed to his parents now that others were going to be involved in the investigation.

Roni shot a quick glance at Heath and in unspoken agreement, she said, "Hopefully we can avoid that. It all depends on your cooperation and what our CSI team finds."

Ricky nodded emphatically. "Whatever you need."

Heath handed Ricky his business card just as Trey and the CSI team walked back into the home. "We're going to leave a squad car here to protect you."

"Why would you do that? The neighbors are going to freak," he said, obviously still worried his parents would become aware of his activities.

Roni shared a look with Heath before she said, "You may be in danger now that we've confirmed this is where the supposed business parties occurred. The officers will be here for your protection and if you have a security system—"

"You think someone will come after me?" he asked, getting even more agitated.

Roni nodded. "We do, Ricky. If you see anything out of the ordinary, you call us immediately and make sure to use the security system."

We do. I'll set it," he said, his face paling at her words.

She nodded. "Good. We'd like to see you later today at the station house. We'll arrange for the officers who are here to bring you in for the lineup and other testing."

Ricky scanned the card and said, "I have a remote class at two, but can be there at three."

"We'll be waiting for you," Roni said and turned to Trey as he approached. "Anything outside?"

He blew out a rough breath. "Fingerprints on some of the tables and chairs. They're not sure they'll be able to get anything off the statues at this point."

She peered at the CSI team as they headed to the upstairs floor of the home. "I'm not sure they'll get much inside. The home has been thoroughly cleaned, except for Ricky's room."

Which made her think to ask, "Do you stay for these parties, Ricky?"

He shook his head. "No. I stay with my girlfriend whenever I rent out the house."

"She can confirm that?" Trey asked.

Ricky once again whitened and his voice was shaky as he said, "Like are you asking if I have an alibi? Do I need an alibi?"

Roni placed a hand on his arm to calm him. "We just need to know if you were here for the parties."

"I wasn't. I thought they were just business parties," he said again and relaxed, but only a little bit, obviously still worried about the fact that a crime had possibly happened in his family home and that his parents would discover that.

She bit back the fact that honest businesses didn't pay in cash for things like that, which reminded her about something else. "Come to think of it, since you're now in business renting this home, you might want to be sure you're doing things like getting the right licenses, paying taxes. That kind of thing, you know."

"S-s-sure. I will," Ricky stammered although she suspected it would be a long time, if ever, that he rented out the home again.

With a jerk of her thumb toward Heath and Trey, she said, "We'll be going, but our CSI team may be here a little longer. We'll see you at three."

Ricky nodded. "I'll be there."

Chapter Twenty

"You need to meet me right now. I'll be on the first floor of the parking lot," he snapped off, worried that Walsh, idiot that he was, had created a trail leading straight to Santana and from Santana to him. With each step closer to him, the body count was growing but it was either that or execution by lethal injection. Too many bodies to avoid the needle.

Unless he ran, which was a real possibility. He had enough tucked away, but it would mean leaving his ex-wife and kids behind. He wouldn't miss the ex-wife, but not seeing his kids would tear his heart out.

Is it better for them to know their father sold women into slavery and murdered a cop and others? the little voice in his head challenged.

He ignored his conscience because he didn't intend to be caught.

Hiding in the alcove leading to the stairs in the parking lot, he waited for the ding that said an elevator had arrived in the nearby elevator banks. At this time of day, most people were still at work in their offices, and as he sneaked a quick look around, he was pleased to see that no one was in the area.

The ding warned of an arrival. He waited, heart racing in his chest. Palms wet with sweat inside the gloves on the handles of the garrote.

"Damn it," Santana muttered and a second later, a footfall alerted him to Santana's approach, probably as the other man was searching for him.

Santana popped out from the edge of the elevator bank, and he jumped into action, wrapping the wire around Santana's neck.

He pulled it tight before the other man could react.

Santana struggled, eyes bulging, face turning red as he clawed at the wire.

He pulled harder, tugging the wire so tight it cut into flesh, and blood leaked from Santana's neck.

Santana's knees sagged, but he flailed his arms, trying to break the hold on the garrote without any success. Santana's body grew heavy on his arms as his life ebbed away and Santana's last feeble attempts to free himself stopped.

Done, he thought and released the handles of the garrote.

Santana's body fell to the floor, his head hitting the railing by the curb with a sickening thud. Not that it mattered since he was deader than dead.

Ducking into the stairwell, he checked for any CCTV cameras and seeing none, he ripped off the black balaclava he'd been wearing and stuffed it into his jacket pocket. Rushing up the steps from the first floor of the underground garage, he reached the ground floor where he could exit to the street. Aware that there was a camera on a bank across the way, he kept his face turned toward the building so they couldn't get a clear view of him.

He'd parked his car on a camera-free side street a few blocks up, but as he neared his car, his phone rang. He cursed. A call meant phone records that could place him here.

Glancing at the screen, he saw that it was his partner. He muttered another curse and ignored the call.

He'd had business to take care of. Luckily that business was now concluded.

But he wasn't going to be heading back to the station house. It was time to transport his last shipment for his paycheck and then get the heck out of Dodge.

As PROMISED, Ricky Martin showed up at the station house, then gave a statement and successfully identified Walsh in a lineup.

Trey had no doubt that with as much evidence as they'd collected, they'd secure a conviction against Walsh. But that wasn't enough. If Santana was involved, which Trey believed he was, they needed more to be able to arrest him. And of course, there was finding the missing women, discovering who was the dirty cop and proving Doug's innocence. Last, but not least, pushing Roni to explain why she hadn't told him she was supposedly working with IAD.

He was still steaming inside about that, and it made him wonder if he could ever trust her again.

"We need to sweat Walsh again now that Ricky picked him out in the lineup," Trey said as Roni sat with him in the conference room, going over the information Ricky had provided and adding it to their growing pile of evidence. Heath had gone back to his desk to get the information they'd been sent from the medical examiner about the Jane Doe homicide.

"I agree. We've got enough on Walsh to lock him up for a long time. But now we need to press him about everything else, including Doug," Roni said, as she took the pile of papers in her hands and tapped them against the tabletop to straighten the sheets.

Since she'd mentioned Doug, it seemed as if now was as good a time as any to ask her about IAD.

"Why didn't you tell me you were working with Ramirez and Anderson?"

Bright color erupted on her cheeks and her grip on the papers faltered, forcing her to try and straighten the papers again.

"Like I told you at the church. You're family," she urged, voice cracking with emotion. But was it guilt?

"Funny way to treat *familia*. Did you doubt my innocence?" he pushed.

"Never," she answered without hesitation, and he actually believed her. "But like I already told you, Ramirez is not your fan. Even though he said there was nothing against you, I worried he could twist whatever he had."

"And you didn't trust me to be able to handle Ramirez?" he said, angry that she hadn't trusted him to know what to do about the biased IAD detective.

"It's not about trust—"

"Obviously not since I don't know if I can trust you anymore, Roni," he shot back.

The color on her cheeks fled as she paled to a sickly white. "You really think that?" she asked, her voice barely above a whisper. Her hands almost strangling the papers she had in her hands.

He'd hurt her because he had been hurt to find out about her actions. But was it unfair? Throughout the entire investigation she'd shown him that she was determined to find out who had shot him and killed his partner. *She's had my back*, he reminded himself.

"I know you meant well…"

"I wanted to keep you safe and find out what had happened to Doug," she choked out.

"Doug," he blew out a breath and dove his hand into his hair. "We still have no idea why Walsh was with Doug or who put the money into that account."

"Nothing from Sophie or Robbie yet?" Roni asked, voice slightly stronger. She stuffed the papers into their case file.

"They texted late last night. Whoever did the hacking is really good. They think they'll be able to identify the where, but not the who," he said and shook his head.

"The 'where' as in Russia or China?" she asked, knowing they were two of the world's worst countries for hacking.

"They're definitely in the top ten. China is also one of the worst countries for human trafficking, but the trafficking usually originates in China to provide cheap labor and sex workers to other countries," he explained.

Roni shook her head. "We're going to stop them here. And we're going to find those missing college students."

"We are," he said, wanting to reassure her.

The door burst open without warning as Heath rushed in. "Dispatch just got a call about a homicide at MCP Enterprises. They found Santana dead in the parking garage. Homicide was just about to head out, but I stopped them in case you want me to go with them."

Trey nodded and shot to his feet. "Go with them and keep us posted."

"I will," Heath said and hurried off into the squad room.

"We need to get Walsh into the box now. Whoever killed Santana is tidying up loose ends. That means they're either going to move those women or kill them," Roni said and hurried to the phone to call the holding cell officer to bring up Walsh since he had not yet been transferred to the local jail.

Trey nodded. "I agree."

As they walked out of the conference room, Trey caught sight of Ramirez barreling his way toward them. Trey jerked back his shoulders, regretting it instantly as pain erupted at the spot where he was still healing from the gunshot.

When Ramirez stopped in front of them, Trey straightened up a notch. "Ramirez. What can we do for you today?" he said, tone chilly.

"Have you seen Anderson? I wanted him here to watch your lineup with Walsh, but he's been MIA all day," the other detective said.

Trey and Roni shared a look and Ramirez didn't fail to pick up on it. "What's going on?"

"Walsh's boss is dead. Sergeant Williams is on his way with Johnson and Tomaso from the homicide department," Trey advised and jammed his hands into his pockets.

Ramirez muttered a curse and seemed about to say something, but then clenched his lips shut.

"You know something you're not sharing," Roni said, picking up on his demeanor.

Another curse burst from his mouth before he said, "We've got nothing more on your partner Adams, but along the way...something was rubbing me wrong."

"About...?" Trey pushed.

At that moment, the uniformed officer came up with Walsh.

With a jerk of his head, Trey gestured for the officer to take Walsh into the interrogation room, despite Walsh's protests.

Sticking his head out of the room as the officer tried to take him in, Walsh shouted, "I want my lawyer!"

"We're getting him," Trey shouted back, although he had no intention of waiting for the attorney when lives were at stake.

Trey jabbed a finger in Ramirez's chest and said, "We're not done here."

Ramirez brushed aside Trey's finger. "I'm going to watch the interview."

When he walked away, Roni said, "Anderson's missing and Santana's dead. You thinking what I'm thinking?"

"I am, and we should use that to our advantage. Do you agree?" Trey asked, pausing by the closed door to the interrogation room.

"I do. He has to know that if Santana is dead and Anderson's gone, he's the one who's going to hang for all these crimes," Roni said, hand poised on the door handle.

"I'll tell him about Santana and let you do the honors about Anderson," he said.

Roni nodded and they walked into the interrogation room.

"You can't talk to me without my attorney," Walsh repeated.

"Like I said before, we're getting him, and in the meantime, we're recording so he can't object to anything that happens. But we have some news to share with you that couldn't wait," Trey said and shot a quick look at Roni before he fixed his gaze to watch Walsh's face as he delivered the news.

"We just got a call. It seems as if Santana—your boss—is dead. They found his body in the parking lot. Possible homicide."

Walsh reared back from the table and his face paled to the color of a seasick sailor. "D-d-dead? Homicide?"

"Looks that way. We're waiting for a report from our partner, but the first officers on the scene called for Homicide and CSI," Trey advised.

Walsh gripped the edges of the table as if to steady himself. Sweat had broken out on his upper lip and his skin had yet to regain any color.

Definitely time for the second salvo. With the barest hint of a nod, Roni picked up on Trey's instruction.

"We know that one of our officers is involved with you and Santana. We also know who it is—Ian Anderson," Roni lied, hoping Walsh's response would confirm Anderson was the dirty cop and not Ramirez.

The green tint to his skin grew even deeper and Walsh's hands were so tight on the edge of the table she worried he'd leave marks on the surface. "I want my lawyer," he eked out, throat almost choked shut with emotion.

"Hopefully he'll be here soon. And hopefully while we wait for him Anderson won't either move or kill those girls. If he does—"

"I'm not responsible for Anderson!" Walsh shouted and slapped the tabletop, the sound as loud as a gunshot in the small room.

"Are you willing to talk to us without your lawyer now?" Roni asked and Trey admired her cool so they could get usable testimony.

"What do I get if I do?" he said, slightly calmer now that he thought he had something he could trade to help himself.

Trey shared a look with Roni, and she pushed on. "We can speak to the district attorney and let her know you cooperated with us."

"Not enough," Walsh said, chin tilted up brazenly. "I want immunity. Witness protection. The people Anderson answers to are animals. It's why I went to talk to your partner."

"You sought out Doug Adams?" Trey asked, shocked by the fact that it had been Walsh reaching out but pleased.

With a shrug, Walsh said, "I'd seen him around. He stuck out and I figured him for a cop."

"You reached out to him to do what?" Roni asked, seeing that Trey had been as surprised by the revelation as she had been.

"After one of the girls died from a roofie, I wanted out. She was the one in the photo you showed me. I knew there was only one way to do that if I didn't want to end up dead too," Walsh said.

Roni quickly opened their case file and took out the

selfie with the woman Heath had identified as the possible Jane Doe homicide. She laid the photo in front of Walsh and asked, "Will you confirm that this is the woman who died?"

Walsh nodded, and Roni said, "Did she die the night the two kidnapped sex workers were taken over to Terminal Island?"

He nodded again. "Yes. I never signed up for this."

"But you were okay with selling women into slavery?" Roni said, voice hot with anger.

The first hint of color crept back into his face with Roni's accusation.

"You approached Detective Adams in order to turn yourself in?" Trey asked, wanting to get it on record that his partner had not been involved with any of the wrongdoing.

"I did, but I didn't realize Anderson was also at the club. I think your partner saw him and put two and two together," Walsh explained.

Which cleared his partner, but something wasn't making sense to him, and Roni must have picked up on it also.

"ANDERSON SAW YOU with Adams, but you're still alive. Why is that?" Roni asked.

"Insurance," Walsh immediately responded.

"Meaning?" Roni pushed.

"I sent a statement and evidence to my lawyer to be opened and made public if I should be killed," Walsh said, leaning back in his chair and adopting a more casual pose, arms across his chest.

With the information Walsh had provided so far,

they could nail Anderson, but did Walsh know about the higher-ups? Did he know about where the missing women were? she wondered and forged ahead.

"Where are the two college students you took? They weren't on Terminal Island."

"There wasn't enough room in the storage container for the women from the second party," he said without hesitation.

Roni racked her mind to picture the storage container, which could have easily held more than two women. It hit her then. "You had more than those two women in the container after the first party?"

He nodded. "We had six in there originally, but they got moved out before those two prostitutes were brought in. They weren't part of the original plan, which was why they were still there."

Which meant they might have more than just the two college students at their new location. "How many women did you take at the second party and where are they?"

Chapter Twenty-One

Trey tugged hard on the bottom edge of Roni's bullet-proof vest, making sure it was securely in place.

"Ready?" he asked, although he wasn't sure he was. The kinds of people who would kidnap women and murder cops weren't going to go down easily and while he was feeling much better since leaving the hospital, he wasn't one hundred percent. But he felt well enough to handle this assignment.

"Ready," she said, but as she zipped one of the vest's straps again, her hands were shaking.

He wanted to take her hand into his, but Heath was standing there as well as Captain Rogers and an entire SWAT team since they expected major trouble once they entered the warehouse Walsh had identified as the location where the women were imprisoned.

The SWAT team would be in charge of breaching the location while Rogers oversaw the general operation. Ramirez was also there since Anderson was his partner. They had positioned themselves a block away from the warehouse and were finalizing their plans for their entry into the building.

Lieutenant Barry, the head of the SWAT team, spread

a blueprint of the warehouse across the surface of one of the squad cars for the officers who would be offering backup.

Barry gestured to the blueprint. "We have entrances at three different locations. We will be positioning our men on the nearby rooftops to guard those entrances as well as uniforms as backup."

He tapped a finger at each of the entrances. "Lopez, Gonzalez and Williams can go in at these locations with our team members, but we need to be careful. Our thermal imaging shows suspects near each of these entrances."

Drifting his finger across the blueprint, he identified another enclosed room at the center of the warehouse space. "There is also one suspect outside that secured central area and one inside that area where we have a number of individuals. Hard to tell how many because they're huddled together," he explained.

"You think that huddle is the missing women?" Roni asked and stretched on tiptoes to review the blueprint.

Barry nodded. "We do and we need to be careful to avoid any collateral damage when we breach."

Trey's gut tightened with fear for the kidnapped women as well as Roni and the other officers who would be risking their lives to save them. It brought back to mind the discussion he'd had with his brother Ricky after that fateful night that seemed so long ago.

His brother had asked him if he ever worried about how his family felt every time he'd gone on a deployment or went into the field on a dangerous assignment. He'd brushed it off as he always did, saying it was part of the job, but now, faced with Roni going into danger, it was way harder to call it just a job.

And maybe he understood a little better why his family wanted him safe. Even why they wanted him working with them. But he pushed those thoughts aside to focus on this mission. They had to rescue the women and he had to make sure any danger to Roni was minimal.

He focused intently as Lieutenant Barry continued with the explanation of their breach of the warehouse and the actions that would follow. Every element was precisely laid out, but obviously subject to the uncertainties of how their suspects would react.

They split up into their assigned teams immediately after the briefing and Trey cursed as Roni rushed off with her group. But she looked back at him, eyes wide, and he offered up a reassuring smile and wished that they had had a chance to finally settle the upset between them about her agreeing to work with IAD.

He hoped there would be time enough for that afterward.

Roni moved toward the entrance to the warehouse with the SWAT team members, the two officers a shield in front of her as they reached the entrance and waited for the go-ahead to breach the warehouse.

Her heart pounded in her chest and her hand was wet on the grip of her Glock. Sweat drenched her beneath the bulletproof vest, a combination of Miami heat and humidity and bone-deep fear. For herself. For the officers about to act and the women inside.

For Trey. She'd almost lost him nearly two weeks earlier and she worried about losing him today. Especially now that she had no doubt about her feelings for him.

It wasn't a girl's crush anymore. She was a woman in love with an amazing man. A hero.

But she wasn't sure if he felt the same. He'd been angry about the revelation that she'd agreed to work with IAD. And she was a fellow cop. And Mia's best friend. Was that all too much?

She had no time to think anything else about that as the call came across the wire.

"We breach in three. One. Two. Three."

The two SWAT members rushed through the fatal funnel of the door ahead of her. Gunfire pinged against the metal wall of the warehouse as they moved in and tucked themselves behind some wooden crates right by the door. The MCP Enterprises name was emblazoned on the crates.

Gunfire echoed in the large space from other parts of the warehouse, but she kept her head, searching for their assailant's position.

She spotted him on a staircase a few yards away from them. He was exposed to their fire and so he kept up a steady barrage of bullets as he tried to work his way up the staircase and to a possible escape route on the roof.

Dropping low, she fired and caught the shooter in the leg. He lost his balance and stopped firing as he tried to right himself. It was the perfect opportunity for the one of the SWAT officers to take him out.

With that doorway clear, they pushed forward toward the center of the space where they suspected the women were huddled together. The SWAT officers moved ahead of her, but as they rounded one corner, gunshots rang out again. One of the SWAT members grabbed at his leg and signaled for them to stay back as he sank to the floor.

"How bad?" his team member asked.

"Bad," the man answered as blood spurted from beneath his fingers.

"Officer down," the other officer called out as he reached into the front pocket of his vest and whipped out a tactical first aid kit to assist while Roni took the lead position to keep the shooter from advancing on them.

There was no sign of their shooter, ripping a curse from her. "We lost him," she called out.

Seconds later the uninjured SWAT officer joined her, his teammate's blood on his hands. "He's stable. We have to push forward."

She nodded and he hurried out ahead of her, sweeping his gun back and forth to protect them while the rest of the team reported over the earpieces.

"Team 1 has secured our entrance. Two suspects down."

"Team 2 has secured. One suspect in custody. One down."

"Team 3 not secure. Suspect is still at large," her SWAT officer reported.

"Teams 1 and 2. Thermal showing one possible suspect inside and to the right in the secured central room. Breach on three," Lieutenant Barry said and counted down.

Roni braced herself for the explosion needed to break through any lock on the door and disorient anyone inside the room. Even with that, she jumped at the loud bang of the blast and the clang of the door as it flew open. Gunfire erupted, echoing in the metal walls of the warehouse.

Suddenly the pop of a gunshot rang out and she literally heard the whiz as the bullet zipped by her head.

A rapid succession of gunfire from the SWAT member followed, deafening her for a moment. Her ears were still ringing as she heard in her earpiece, "Suspect down."

Only one suspect left based on the intel they had from the thermal imaging and her count of how many were either down or in custody.

"Central area is secure," someone said.

Breathing out a relieved sigh, she let her guard down.

A mistake as an arm immediately wrapped around her neck and the icy metal of a muzzle kissed her temple.

"Drop it and don't say a word," Anderson said as the SWAT member whirled around, obviously sensing something was wrong.

Holding the weapon and his free hand in a gesture of surrender, he laid it down.

"Kick it here and zip-tie yourself to that shelf," Anderson said, but the other officer hesitated.

"Do it now or I'll blow her brains out," he said, close to the ear with the earpiece, and Roni hoped the others heard what was happening.

The officer did as he asked, but Roni wasn't going down so easily.

"You're not going to get out of here. You know there's backup," she said as he started to walk her backwards toward the entrance.

"They won't risk a shot, Lopez. You should know

that," he said, moving closer and closer to the entrance, but as he did so, Roni noticed motion a few rows away from them.

Trey. Moving toward them and the entrance.

A SWAT officer was hot on his heels, but would they act before Anderson was able to get her outside where they would have to rely on one of their snipers to take him out?

Could they take him out before he killed her? she worried as the pressure of the muzzle against her temple increased.

As they neared the door, Trey slowly stepped out from behind the row of shelves, hands up in a surrender gesture. It caused Anderson to stop short.

"Don't make things worse for yourself, Ian. Surrender," Trey called out.

Anderson laughed harshly. "Worse? They're probably going to get Old Sparky out for me."

"Surrender and we'll talk to the DA. Ask them not to push for capital punishment," he said, although considering how many bodies had piled up, Roni wasn't sure that was a promise Trey could keep.

"On which murder?" Anderson asked, his mind in sync with hers.

A slight movement to her left caught her eye. A SWAT officer possibly moving in for a kill shot. Since the gun on her temple didn't waver, she suspected Anderson hadn't picked up on the motion.

"On all of them, Ian. Cooperate with us. Help us get those running this ring—"

"Who will kill me if I do," Ian shouted, and for the

first time, the muzzle at her temple shifted, maybe far enough away for her to make a move to escape.

But as her gaze met Trey's, she realized it was too late.

The blast of an assault rifle registered a heartbeat before the spray of something warm against the side of her face.

Anderson's arm slipped from around her neck as he dropped to the ground at her feet, a gaping hole in the side of his head, a pool of blood quickly growing on the ground from the fatal wound.

TREY RUSHED TO Roni's side at the sight of the blood across her face and neck and the sickly white of her skin. Her knees buckled just as he got there, but as he slipped an arm around her, she gathered herself. Her muscles trembled beneath his arm, but she straightened and met his gaze directly.

"Are you okay?" he asked, examining her for any signs of injury. Hoping the blood was all Anderson's.

"I'm okay," she said and repeated it almost to convince herself. "I'm okay."

"Last suspect down. Gonzalez and Lopez are coming out the door," erupted across his earpiece as the SWAT officer reported in.

The remaining officers called in to report that they had secured their areas and Lieutenant Barry said, "All clear. Let's get the EMTs in there to check out our victims."

Roni and Trey walked toward one of the squad cars, Trey with his arm around her waist to offer support.

One of the EMTs saw the blood on her face and neck and hurried over.

"I'm okay," Roni said yet again, but the EMT used some gauze to wipe away the blood and confirm that she was in fact uninjured.

They walked to where Rogers and Ramirez waited. Rogers immediately asked, "Anderson?"

Trey shook his head. "SWAT officer took him out."

Ramirez muttered something under his breath and jammed his hands on his hips. "Anderson took the key to this operation to the grave."

Trey couldn't argue with that. "We'll get what we can from Walsh. What's important now is that we freed nearly a half a dozen women."

"I agree, Detective. Since we have things under control here, why don't you and Detective Lopez head home," Rogers said with a bob of his head in Roni's direction.

"Will do, Captain," he confirmed.

"Are you ready, Roni?" he asked. Beneath his arm, her trembling had slowly subsided, replaced by strength.

With a nod, she said, "I'm ready."

Chapter Twenty-Two

Although the threat to their lives was over, they returned to the South Beach Security penthouse apartment rather than returning to their respective homes.

They walked in to find Sophie, Rob and Trey's brother Ricky waiting there for them.

"We heard the news over the police scanner," Ricky said and walked over to hug her and shake Trey's hand.

"The women are safe, but we don't have what we need to track down the ringleaders," Roni said with a sad shake of her head.

Sophie came over and hugged her as well. "You'll find them. They can't hide forever," Sophie said.

Rob joined them to offer his hug. "It may take time, but it will happen."

Roni nodded although she wasn't as confident as Trey's cousins.

"We'll make it happen and to do that, we should get going," Sophie said and after another hug for Roni, she and Rob headed toward the elevator.

"Maybe you should head out as well," Trey said to his brother, earning a raised eyebrow from Ricky.

"Are you sure?" his younger brother asked.

Ricky only wanted to help, but Roni wasn't ready to talk about what had happened. As Ricky glanced her way, she said, "We're sure. Maybe some other time."

He rolled his eyes and mumbled as he walked away, "Just proves women can be as stupidly macho as any man."

After the trio had departed on the elevator, Roni faced Trey. "What do we do now?"

"Shower. Dinner. Maybe talk if you're up to it," he said.

She wasn't sure she was up for the latter, but the first two seemed heavenly.

"Sounds good," she said and hurried off to the shower, needing time alone to process all that had happened in the last few hours.

TREY WATCHED RONI walk away and close the door to her room.

It almost felt like she was closing herself off from him because in the several hours after the rescue at the warehouse, he'd felt the tension and distance growing between them.

He understood. There was so much for them to hash out.

But first, a shower, he thought, until the elevator dinged, opened and his younger brother Ricky appeared again.

"Come on, *hermanito*. I told you I'm not ready to talk to you," Trey said and dragged a hand through his hair in frustration.

"Fine, but I'm ready to talk to you, *hermano*. I know you too well not to see that you are about to mess up the best thing that's ever happened to you," Ricky said and walked over to where Trey was standing by the breakfast bar in the kitchen area.

He settled on one of the stools, clearly determined to have his say.

"If you mean Roni, there's a lot there you can't even begin to understand," Trey said.

"Like the fact that she's another cop? A good one at that? Does that bother you?" Ricky said, more observant than Trey liked. But then again, maybe that's what made him such a good psychologist and more importantly, a wonderful brother.

"Yes, it does, not that I like to admit it," he said.

"Because now you know how the rest of us feel," Ricky challenged.

Trey sighed heavily, feeling the guilt all the way into his soul. "*Sí*, because seeing her with a gun to her head—" he mimicked what he'd seen only hours earlier with his hand "—seeing that made my blood run cold."

Ricky eyed him carefully. "Which I guess means that you care for her."

Trey did a little dip of his head. "I do, but it's even more complicated."

Ricky lifted one dark brow in question. "Tell me more."

Trey looked away and shook his head. "She asked me to trust her, but she didn't tell me she was working with IAD."

"To clear Doug, I assume," Ricky said, sounding way too logical, which in turn made him feel way too unreasonable. He'd been feeling that way ever since he'd lashed out at her and she'd explained why she'd agreed but also that she hadn't really gone through with it.

But only because of circumstances, he thought.

"Trey? You still there?" Ricky pressed.

"I am and I'm still mad only... I know why she did it," Trey admitted.

"What are you going to do about that? About Roni?" Ricky asked, clearly determined to push Trey into action, only Trey wasn't about to be forced into something so important.

"I'm going to think about it and if I need to talk some more, I will reach out to you, *hermanito*," he said as he rose and gestured toward the elevator door.

"I'll hold you to that promise, Trey," Ricky said and walked over to the elevator.

Once he'd left, Trey shut down access from the main floor so that Roni and he would have privacy for the discussion they had to have.

A discussion that he didn't know how to begin and worse, how to end.

He still had too many conflicting emotions about all that had happened between them, but they had to clear the air because today had confirmed one thing to him.

He loved Roni Lopez. He only hoped she felt the same.

RONI UNDRESSED AND tossed her bloodied shirt into the trash. She didn't think she could ever wear it again without remembering the muzzle at her temple and the warm spray of Anderson's blood.

It could have just as easily been her blood. It could have been her lying dead on the floor.

A chill filled her again and her muscles trembled with those thoughts. She wrapped her arms around her waist, trying to steady herself as she headed into the bathroom.

She got the water running as hot as she could stand it, stepped beneath the spray and stood there for long minutes, washing away the blood and memories. The heat of the water warmed her and drove away the earlier chill in her core.

When her body finished shaking, she washed, luxuriating in the silken feel of the soap against her skin. She almost didn't want to leave the shower because she knew that once she went back out into the suite, Trey and she were going to have to talk.

Her gut clenched again at that realization, but she took a steadying breath and finished up her shower. She could only delay for so long and her fingers were getting wrinkly from her long soak.

She slipped on a loose T-shirt and sweats, needing comforting things for what might possibly be a difficult discussion.

As she stepped out into the main area of the suite, the rich smell of coffee filled her nostrils.

Trey was at the kitchen counter, his back to her. Like her, he'd slipped into a T-shirt and sweats that hung loose on his lean hips.

He half turned as she came in, and he said, "It's late. I know I need a little pick-me-up."

"I do, too." They'd grabbed a vending machine dinner at the precinct, but very little could make her drink the toxic brew that passed for coffee at the office.

She walked to his side and watched as he deftly

steamed some milk and poured it into the mugs with the coffee. He handed her a mug and she walked over to the sofa in the center of the suite.

Settling onto the couch, she tucked her legs beneath her and sipped her coffee as he joined her, sitting at the opposite end of the couch. Just as she had done, he sipped his coffee and kept silent. The tension built between them, like a balloon being slowly inflated, and she waited for it to reach that point where it would just pop.

And then it happened.

"I should be furious with you," he said and set his mug on the coffee table in front of the sofa.

"Should be? Does that mean you're not?" she asked, hoping that he'd seen reason about why she'd agreed to work with IAD.

He shrugged, crossed his arms against his chest and tucked his hands under his armpits, as if to keep himself from reaching for her. If he did, she didn't know if she could keep from touching back. When he hesitated, she asked again, "You're not furious?"

Shaking his head, he said, "When I saw Anderson had you…a million thoughts went through my brain."

"I wish I could say the same. My mind went blank," she said with a heavy sigh. She pushed back a wet lock of hair that fell forward as she looked away from him.

She heard the creak of the leather on the couch a second before she caught sight of his thigh coming to rest against her knees. He tucked his thumb and index finger beneath her chin and applied gentle pressure to urge her gaze up to his.

"You might say that, but I know that you were thinking about what to do every second. I was proud of you, Roni, but also more scared than I ever imagined I could be," he said and stroked his thumb across her lips, the gesture as intimate as a caress.

Relieved that this was going way better than she ever could have imagined, she said, "So you're not mad."

"I am mad. I'm mad that you even thought about working with IAD without telling me. I'm mad that you risked your life," he said. She was about to argue, but he laid his thumb against her lips to silence her.

"Don't tell me that's what cops do. I know that. And as my brother Ricky wisely reminded, that's how my family feels about me being a cop," he said and drifted his hand back to tangle his fingers in the wet strands of her hair.

Holding her steady, he leaned close and brushed a butterfly kiss across her lips. "I don't want to lose you, Roni. I love you."

She smiled and whispered, "And I love you, Trey."

She kissed him and dug her hands into his hair, caressing his head as their mouths met over and over, the kiss deepening with each breath they took until they were both trembling with need.

But she wanted more and shifted back to meet his gaze, heavy with desire. "While the sofa was great last time—"

"I want to spend the entire night in your bed," he said with a sexy, boyish grin, his ocean blue eyes alight with joy.

She smiled. "I like that we can agree on that," she said, as she rose and held her hand out to him.

He slipped his hand into hers, stood and followed her into the bedroom.

She was grateful she'd worn the loose, casual clothing since he quickly had her naked beside him. Luckily, it took only a few tugs, and he was out of his T-shirt and sweatpants and backing her toward the bed.

Her knees hit the side of the mattress and he urged her to sit, and before she knew it, he was between her legs, kissing her. Making her body jump with the lick and tug of his mouth.

The climax slammed into her, unexpected and so strong, her vision swam.

"I'm here, *amor mio*," he said and helped her shift into the center of the bed.

With a kiss as her senses realigned, he said, "I'll be back."

Protection, she thought as he rushed back and climbed onto the bed beside her.

HER BODY QUAVERED beside him, still coming down from the powerful release that had ripped through her just moments before.

He wanted to feel that release. Feel her as she came back to earth before he would take her to the edge again and go over with her.

Tenderly easing over her body, he positioned himself at her center as she opened to him. Slowly, almost hesitantly, he slipped inside her. Experienced the feel of her body accepting him. Surrounding him and cradling him as she wrapped her arms and legs around him to complete their union.

"Why did we wait so long?" he said and groaned,

gritting his teeth as his release rose up faster than he had imagined.

She kissed him and whispered against his lips. "Shut up and kiss me."

He did, over and over. His mouth mobile against hers as he moved in her and she matched him. The two of them rising ever higher, reaching together, until with one last thrust, they tumbled over the edge together.

TREY'S BIG BODY shuddered one last time and he braced himself on his arms to keep his weight off her, but she urged him down, wanting his weight. Wanting that connection of their bodies joined together.

The aftermath of their climax ebbed leisurely, and he finally shifted to his side, but laid his big hand across her midsection to maintain the connection.

She placed her hand over his and stroked it, gentling him, but feeling a rising tension in his body that had worry erupting in hers. Shifting to her side, she faced him and stroked a hand across his chest. Beneath her palm his heartbeat was slowing, returning to normal. But she sensed that growing strain in his body once more.

"Please don't say you regret this," she said, again passing her hand across his chest.

He laid his hand over hers and stilled her movement. "Never, *mi amor*. I love you and I want this to go somewhere."

"Somewhere?" she asked, confused by his choice of words.

"I know this isn't normal. We haven't even been on a date—we've just known each other forever."

"We have. At least ten years," she said.

He brushed his fingers across her cheek, a wistful smile on his face. "You were such a baby when you came home with Mia and Carolina."

She chuckled and cupped his jaw. His beard was rough as sandpaper beneath her palm. "And you were the big college freshman. I have to confess that when I saw you in your Marine uniform for that ROTC dance, I was kind of jealous of the girl you were taking."

Trey's smile broadened and he slipped his hand behind her neck to draw her close for a kiss. "I still have my uniform and I'm ready to dance when you are."

"Unfortunately, I have two left feet," she said with a twisted smile.

"I'm sure we can work on that," Trey said, his gaze gleaming with promise, but then he turned serious. "That is, if you want this to be more."

If I want it to be more? How many times have I imagined just that? she thought.

"It will be tough with both of us being cops. The hours are crazy," she said and dropped another kiss on his lips.

"*Sí*, it would be only… The night I was shot I saw my parents. The worry had made them look years older."

She heard what he wasn't saying and was surprised. Cupping his cheek, she touched him tenderly, aware of how hard it would be for him to say it. "They love you. They worry. We all worry," she said.

He tapped her nose playfully. "You worry and I do, too. Today was more of an eye-opener than I expected," he confessed.

She'd be lying if she denied that almost being killed

hadn't made an impact. She'd been in danger before, but nothing like today. "It was…scary," she said, and as it sank in, her body trembled again and grew cold, as if reliving that fear.

"It was," he said and tightened his hold on her, drawing her close until every inch of their bodies was in contact. The strength and warmth of his body helped drive away the chill and quivering.

"I've finally heard what my family is saying. And now I've seen all they can do to help those who we might not be able to get help from the police…" His voice trailed off, but she knew what he wasn't saying.

"They've wanted you to join South Beach Security for years," she said and skimmed her hand lightly over the angry scar at his shoulder.

"They have and maybe it's time to do that," he said, finally confessing to what had been in his mind, even though he'd seemed to be dead set against it.

But he'd almost died barely two weeks ago. Doug *had* died.

And today, she'd nearly been killed, only she wasn't sure she was ready to leave the force.

"They'll be happy to hear that, Trey," she said.

"They will and I hope that'll mean a more normal life for us, Roni. One with kids. I'm not getting any younger, you know," he teased.

"Kids?" she said, thinking he was putting the cart before the horse. "I'm an old-fashioned girl in some ways. Marriage usually comes before kids."

He chuckled and rolled, trapping her beneath his body. It made her all too aware that he was more than ready to work on making kids. "Veronica Lopez. Are you asking me to marry you?" he teased.

She couldn't contain her laugh. "Being a modern woman, I guess I am. Ramon Gonzalez, the third, Trey, will you marry me?"

"I will," he said and kissed her. As he trailed a line of kisses down her neck and to her breasts, both their cell phones started blaring from the other room.

In unison they muttered curses and flew off the bed to answer.

With his longer legs, Trey reached his phone first. "Captain?" he said at the same time that she heard her partner say, "The captain said to track you down."

"I'm here with Trey. We were having…a late dinner," she said, but not very convincingly.

"Yeah, well. I'll let you go back to…eating," Heath said and hung up.

Trey hadn't said a word since picking up, but then he said, "We'll be there shortly, Captain."

"What is it?" she asked as soon as Trey had ended the call.

"Walsh wasn't the only one with insurance. Homicide found evidence in Santana's office that they think we should see."

Chapter Twenty-Three

Trey laid out the photos on the surface of the conference room table while Roni read the journal that Santana had locked in his company's safe.

The homicide squad had found the materials there after executing a search warrant on the premises despite the objections of Santana's lawyer as well as the twentysomething son.

"He's laid out everything in this journal. Every payment. Every delivery of women. Names, but not the leaders of the ring," Roni said as she flipped through the pages.

"And these photos. He paid his own private investigator to document some of the transfers between Anderson and his contacts. Eastern European, possibly Russian, from the looks of them," Trey said as he examined the photos.

Roni nodded and said, "The men on Terminal Island were hired hands, but not Russian. Some of the ones in the warehouse yesterday were. We could tell from the tattoos."

"But we didn't have anything on them in our databases. Hopefully Interpol can help with the photos we sent them. We'll send these as well," he said, gathering all the photos together to scan them and send them to their international partners.

"Let's get to work so we can head home and finish what was so rudely interrupted," Roni said with a sexy smile.

"I'm all in favor of that."

TREY'S AND RONI'S families gathered around them in the penthouse suite as the news reporter announced the upcoming segment on how the police had broken up an international human trafficking ring and solved the murder of a Miami detective and several others, including Sylvia Reyes from the DA's office. Her body had been found, not far from where Anderson had apparently dumped Eddie's body.

The photos of the dead Russian suspects from the warehouse combined with Santana's photos had tied their case to an investigation Interpol had been conducting. Interpol had identified the ringleader, a Russian oligarch whose money and political power had helped him avoid prosecution for years. But with the materials that they had gathered, Interpol felt they finally had enough to go after him.

Roni and he, as well as Sophie and Rob, had been coordinating with Interpol for the last few days, providing them every bit of evidence on the money transfers, kidnappings and murders. Interpol had been confident that the money transfers had been orchestrated by the oligarch's hackers. Walsh, to their chagrin, had been placed in witness protection since his testimony would assist with the prosecution of the oligarch.

With all that done, their investigation was essentially over, but that only meant his life together with Roni could begin including some therapy sessions with Ricky to handle all that had happened with his partner's death and his shooting.

He gripped Roni's hand as the news came on and the reporter introduced the segment. He did a rundown of the case and then the video interview with Roni and ADA Morales popped onto the screen.

"We're very happy to have provided Interpol key information that will assist with their investigation. We're hopeful that with that evidence, Interpol will be able to arrest the leader of this human trafficking ring," Roni stated.

The reporter on the scene turned to ADA Morales, who added her thoughts. "This is a big step in ending the horrible blight of human trafficking in Miami-Dade County. We are hopeful that with the wonderful work of our police department, we can continue to eliminate this plague."

The interview ended and returned to the on-air reporter. "Wonderful progress on a horrible problem in Miami-Dade," he said and then proceeded to the next news story.

The gathered family members clapped, and Mia and Carolina did a big "woo." Trey figured this was as good a time as any for Roni and him to give the families their news.

He tightened his hold on her hand and together they came to their feet for the announcement.

He looked around at his family, including his grandfather and grandmother. Even at 87 his *abuelo* was impressive, sitting ramrod straight in one of the chairs, his almost birdlike wife at his side. Not that his *abuela* should be underestimated. She'd steered her family out of Cuba and kept it together while his grandfather had gone off to the Bay of Pigs and after, to Vietnam. She'd handled the burdens of being married to a police officer and the struggles to build South Beach Security.

Trey was of that strong stock, and he took his strength from that as he glanced at Roni and said, "We have some news for you."

Another "woo" and clapping came from Mia and Carolina who in unison said, "We knew it. We knew you were right for each other."

"Way to kill the surprise," Roni said with a roll of her eyes at her friends' antics.

"Is this true, *mi'jo*?" his father asked, a stern look on his face. He shot a quick look over to Roni's parents and her younger brother, who sat nearby. Roni's dad did a determined nod and smiled.

"It is, Mr. Gonzalez. I proposed to Trey—"

"She proposed! You go, girl," Mia said with a laugh and high-fived Carolina.

"I apologize for not asking for your permission," Roni said with a laugh.

His father shook his head and said, "Modern women."

It earned him an elbow from his very modern wife. "He's lucky to have her and may I just say on behalf of the family, we're very happy that you'll be part of our family, Roni. Soon I hope."

Trey laughed and said, "I warned you they were a tough audience."

Roni playfully swung his hand. "As soon as we can

arrange some things. Trey," she said, guiding him to make the next big announcement.

"Roni and I talked about it and having two police officers in a family would be difficult. Because of that, I was hoping that you'd consider letting me join South Beach Security," Trey said.

The response was nothing like he might have imagined.

His father and grandfather jumped to their feet and rushed over to embrace him and Roni. A second later, his mother and grandmother, the Twins, Ricky and his cousins surrounded them.

They embraced, laughed, kissed and broke apart one by one until it was only his father and grandfather standing by them, smiles beaming from their faces. His father clapped his back and said, "Trey, welcome to South Beach Security. Roni, welcome to our family."

Another "woo" erupted from the Twins, Ricky and his cousins, while the rest of the family gathered around them, clapping and wiping away tears.

As his father and grandfather stepped away, Trey turned to Roni and said, "Are you sure you can deal with all this?"

Roni smiled, rose on tiptoe and whispered against his lips, "For you, I could deal with anything. I love you."

"I love you, too, Roni," he said and kissed her.

As his boisterous family cheered yet again, he smiled and could feel Roni's smile against his lips as well.

He knew then that no matter what, they'd be able to handle everything together.

* * * * *

Look for the next book in New York Times
bestselling author Caridad Piñeiro's
South Beach Security miniseries
when Brickell Avenue Ambush
goes on sale in January!

HARLEQUIN
PLUS

Announcing a **BRAND-NEW** multimedia subscription service for romance fans like you!

Read, Watch and Play.

Experience the easiest way to get the romance content you crave.

Start your **FREE 7 DAY TRIAL** at
www.harlequinplus.com/freetrial.